I'm Gonna Live My Life Like A Jimmy Buffett Song

Thank you, Jimmy, for showing us the doors to so many possible adventures; it's up to the rest of us to dance through them.

Our lives are funny things. We spend so much time worrying about something we've done in the past or trying to plan for the future that we forget all about the now. And that's really a shame because the now is the only place our lives are actually happening. If you don't believe me, try jumping from Monday morning to Friday night without doing all those pesky mundane weekday moments in between, and you'll see what I mean.

Living your life is a lot like traveling. If you get in your car and drive from New York to Los Angeles you don't see Pennsylvania, Ohio, and Indiana all at once, because we haven't figured out yet how to be in two places at the same time. You are where you are and that's that. What we need in life is a big flashing sign that says *"You are here"* to remind us, so we stop looking forwards and backwards all the time. And we need to stop staring at the damn GPS.

I'm not saying there's anything wrong with having a clue where you want to go to in life. But the trick is to not get too hung up on it, and to be ready for some detours along the way. Because some roads are going to be closed no matter what you try to do, and there are always going to be new ones to explore.

Take me for example; when I was a kid I decided I wanted to be an architect. I just knew I was going to design fantastic buildings, changing the Minneapolis skyline to look like something out of Star Trek. It was my destiny; so of course I ended up in Public Relations.

What went wrong along the way? Well, I hit a big ol' pothole; math. I'd always imagined that being an architect meant drawing cool pictures of buildings, which I was very good at, and passing them along to a construction company and saying, *"Build this."* Nobody every bothered telling me I was going to have to be able to calculate whether or not the thing would stay up the first time a stiff breeze blew against it. Simple long division gave me a headache, and if I had to do calculus, it was likely going to blow the top of my head clean off. So while in my case the road to being an architect wasn't really closed, it looked pretty damned bumpy to me, not to mention steep, and I didn't have nearly enough horsepower to tow my lazy ass up that hill.

So like most American high school graduates, I trudged off to college not having any idea what the hell I was doing there, besides drinking and trying to meet women. And it only took me two and a half years and a healthy start on my student loan debt to realize that no matter how many general ed classes I took to stall for time, I was going to continue to just drive around and around the block and get nowhere. Something had to be done before I ended up with a double major in French and French poetry (yes, I was still trying to meet girls). So I pulled into my guidance counselor's office and asked for directions.

Now I know because I'm a guy that asking for directions went against one of our holiest of codes. Looking back, I can see I paid the price for violating it for years. And you should never trust a counselor of any kind. Plug the word *lawyer* into any online thesaurus for example and see what comes back. My counselor was only doing her job. But like Cool Hand Luke said, *"Calling it your job, boss, don't make it right."* Yes, my aptitude tests showed I should be good at PR. And yes, they were right. And yes, I graduated three years later and went straight to work for Image Makers, a large, prestigious, and very boring public relations firm in Minneapolis that worked with corporations to make them seem more loveable. And nine years later I had a nice big car, a nice sized paycheck, a not so nice skinny, blonde girlfriend, and a condo full of Ikea furniture. But like the man said, that don't mean it was right, boss.

So what am I trying to say with all this? I don't have a clue, and I don't want one. To figure that out once and for all would mean dwelling on the past, and

I'm trying to kick the habit. But there is one time to look back without fondly remembering something, and that's to tell a story. And you could say my story, my *real* story, starts more or less here, nine years into the public relations gig my guidance counselor steered me into, sitting inside my condo with the Ikea furniture and my not so nice, skinny, blonde girlfriend.

Chapter 1:
"It's Monday, and it's not all right."

The sun wasn't shining, the birds weren't singing, and it was colder than hell outside my dining room window. A steady snow had been falling since around midnight and had blanketed everything in a frosty white, and I was glad once again that I lived in a condo so at least someone else would have to shovel the crap out of my driveway.

January wasn't my favorite month of the year. In Minnesota it meant we were still knee deep in the heart of winter, even though it had already been hanging around long enough to become a very unwelcome guest. On this particular January day I had my nose buried in the Minneapolis Tribune, a cup of coffee in my hand, trying to shake the cobwebs off. It was a Monday morning so it was slow going, but I was managing to enjoy my last bit of weekend free time before leaving for work.

As usual that didn't last long.

"Jack."

I turned to the sports section to see if there was any interesting lingering news on the Vikings, who had managed to miss the playoffs once again this year.

"Ja-ack..."

There was nothing there, so I skipped over to the comics, hoping Calvin and Hobbs had finally decided to make a comeback, but found no joy yet again.

"Jack!"

I sighed behind my paper, then looked over the top of it at my soul mate, Brittany. "Yes, honey?"

"Do you have to do that?" she said.

"Do what?" I asked, knowing full well what she was going to say.

"Read the paper at the table," she said.

"No, I could read it in the living room instead, if it would make you happy," I said, knowing it would me.

"That's not what I meant, and you know it," she said. "Why do you always have to be such a smart ass?"

"I don't know, but I could go try and find the answer and get back to you," I said.

"Never mind," she said surlily.

"Okay," I said, and went back to my paper.

"Jack!" she snapped.

I looked back over the paper again. "Yes, dear?"

"I wasn't finished!" she said.

"My mistake," I said, putting the paper down on the table in a show of defeat and submission. "What do you want to talk about?"

"Tonight," she said.

I racked my brain, but failed to come up with any reason tonight would be worth interrupting my morning read. "Sorry, drawing a blank here."

"Dinner?" she said.

I thought again, then shook my head. "Still got nothing."

"With my parents?" she said, obviously incredulous that I could have forgotten something so monumental.

"Ah," I said. "*That* dinner."

"Yes, that dinner. The one I've been planning for weeks," said Brittany.

"Out of curiosity, how could you have been planning another night with your parents for weeks, when we just had dinner with them last Tuesday?" I said.

"Look, just be home on time," she said in the tone I loved so much. "We have reservations at Wong's at seven and I don't want to be late; you know how much Daddy hates waiting."

"Hitler probably did too," I said, in my head and to myself where the ensuing argument wouldn't make me late for work. I looked out the window at the thick snow that was still falling. "Do we have to do it tonight?" I said out loud, again knowing full well the

answer, but going through the motions anyway. "It's going to be miserable driving in this stuff."

"Yes, tonight. Daddy's busy the rest of the week," she said.

"*Meeting with the rest of his lawyer buddies to work on their plan for world domination, no doubt,*" I thought, but again holding my tongue. "Fine," I said out loud, resigning myself to a full Monday from hell. I looked at my watch. Usually I wouldn't leave so early, but with Brittany and the weather behaving as they were, it seemed like a good idea to get the heck out of there. "I gotta run." I stood up and walked over and tried to give Brittany a peck on the cheek, but she was busy ignoring me, engrossed in her horoscope now that she'd managed to steal my paper. I shrugged, then grabbed my coat and keys and walked out the door.

There are few things more beautiful than a fresh snowfall out in the country. It's almost magical; crystal icicles hanging from every green tree branch, a glittering, sugary, white blanket covering the ground. The world sparkles like diamonds in the chilly, clear air. For lack of a better word, it looks so...clean.

Not so a citified snow. It's dirty, messy, and damned slippery. Nothing glitters, except maybe the ice that likes to build up on your windshield as you try to drive. And despite the fact that most Minnesotans have driven in the stuff repeatedly throughout their lives, a snowfall always managed to turn a chunk of them into moronic, uncoordinated, driving school rejects.

This winter's morning was no different. On average my commute time to work or back was twenty-five minutes, but it was obviously going to take a lot longer today with all the slide, stop, and go traffic on the freeway. To make matters worse there was a fender bender on Highway 94 and the gawkers were slowing things down even further, seizing this incredibly exciting, once in a lifetime opportunity to see a dented car.

As traffic skidded to an abrupt halt again I swore and tapped on the brakes and brought my Suburban to a dead stop. I sat there for a few seconds wondering who the hell did what up the road this time, then leaned back and started thinking again. I did some of my best thinking in my car (and some of my best swearing too). And it was usually about work (as was a good portion of the swearing). But today my thought topic was Brittany.

We'd been a couple for almost two years now, and had been sharing my condo for just over one. Moving in together had seemed like a good idea at the time; she was a very pretty blonde, at least prettier than a guy like me thought he deserved, and I'd been anxious to get her into my house with the rest of my things before I lost her to someone else. The first six months of cohabitation had gone well enough, but lately I felt like nothing more than an ATM that got abused if it didn't kick out money in a timely enough fashion. That and we never seemed to do anything *I* wanted to do anymore, or even anything *we* wanted to do. It was mostly what *she* wanted to do, like all the constant damned dinners with her parents.

But I wasn't sure I should risk bringing us up again. The last time I'd tried that Brittany had pulled marriage out of her holster, so obviously her guns were a lot bigger than mine. All I was packing was a few wasted hours with her mom and dad and a couple hundred dollars a month lost to the mall. So I'd ducked and run for cover, and didn't have sex for a week as a penalty for my cowardice.

As traffic started moving again I decided to just let it lie. I told myself that if I wasn't going to break up with her and I wasn't going to marry her, both at least for the moment, then there wasn't any point in rocking the boat. It would work itself out one way or another, which was pretty much how I approached everything in my life I wasn't entirely happy about; just leave it alone and hope it got better by itself. Of course most things never did, but that didn't stop me from believing the theory was a sound one.

Besides, as traffic started moving I realized I had a bigger problem on my hands, or at least a more immediate one. Even though I was finally past the dinged up car sideshow, the damage had already been done; between the gawkers and the winter impaired drivers there was no way I was going to make it to work on time. Which meant that unless I was incredibly lucky and my boss, Mr. Ronald Strickland, wasn't watching the office like a deranged hawk with nothing better to do, the first thing I was going to hear as I walked in the door was...

Chapter 2:
"Now it's my job to clean up this mess."

"Danielson! Get your ass in my office!"

Surprisingly I'd made it all the way to the closet and managed to hang up my coat before I heard the scream; my boss was obviously slipping. I trudged my way through the maze of cubicles, getting a thumbs up from my friend Marty as I went past, then went inside the big room.

The head of Image Makers was Mr. Ronald Strickland, a man with no redeeming qualities whatsoever. This was the guy who had fired Bill Reynolds at the company Christmas party a couple of months ago because he wasn't acting jolly enough while playing Santa (Bill's mother had passed away a few days before). He was also the man with a paperweight on his desk with an inscription that read *"Slavery may have been abolished, but I haven't been."* And he was the man who made a point of criticizing every little thing I did, even though *I* knew that *he* knew that I was the best PR person in the firm. If King George would have had me on his side, the U.S. would still be part of England's empire.

I stood in the middle of Mr. Strickland's large, plush, corner office overlooking the Mississippi River, and waited for him to acknowledge my presence. It was one of his favorite tactics; I'm sure he'd read in some corporate power magazine that it gave him the upper hand in the conversation to come if he made me wait. I passed the time by counting the S*uccess, Victory,* and *Achievement* golf pictures he had hanging on his walls; he was up to nine now, having added *Commitment* since my last visit. He only needed *Death To All Who Oppose* to finish his collection.

I suppose since I wasn't doing anything at the moment that it would have been as good a time as any to describe to you what I look like, but I've decided I'm not going to, here or anytime else. The reason I'm not gonna do it is because I think it'd be far more interesting to let you use your own imagination and make me look however you want. So go ahead, I can take it; do your worse. But if you'd like to use said imagination to make me look like, oh, say, George Clooney, somewhen around *The Perfect Storm* era, be my guest; I often do so myself. Thankfully it turns out your imagination won't break no matter how far you stretch the thing.

Mr. Strickland finally finished doing whatever it was he was pretending to do on his computer, and turned his head to face me. "Danielson!" he snapped, which happens to be my last name (and before you ask, no, I'm not from Tennessee, and no, JD is not my father). "You were late today, weren't you?"

"Yes, I know. I'm sorry about that, sir," I said. "There was an accident on 94 and-"

"I don't want to hear any excuses! You're an adult; act like one," said Mr. Strickland, in his finest condescending tone. "With the weather the way it is you should have left for work early."

I wanted to tell him that I *had* left for work early this morning, but given the fact he had just told me he didn't want to hear any excuses, I guessed he probably didn't want to hear that particular one either. "I'm sorry, it won't happen again," I said.

"See that it doesn't," said Mr. Strickland.

"Yes, sir," I said, and turned to leave the office, assuming my buttocks were done being chewed for now.

"Where are you going?" he growled.

I stopped and turned, then smartly said, "Uh..."

"I'm not finished yet," said Mr. Strickland.

"Sorry," I said, for the third time, which was nowhere near my record for a single office visit. I waited to see what he could find to further damage my derriere with.

He looked at me for a moment as if trying to decide where to attack next, then said, "Have a seat."

This was a new tactic. I had never been asked to sit in his office before, which I figured was so that my fanny would remain exposed and vulnerable. Frankly I was a little worried, but sat down in one of the chairs facing his desk.

He studied me again, then said, "How have you been, Jack?"

Now I was really nervous. Not only was he asking me how I was, as if there was some miniscule chance he might actually care, but he was also calling me by my first name, something else he had never before done. "I've been good," I lied.

"That's great," he said. "And your job? Do you like working here?"

"Yes. Yes, I do," I said, my lies growing exponentially as we talked.

"That's great," said Mr. Strickland. "It's important to like your work." He looked at me again, then picked up his gold pen and began tapping it on his desk in a most annoying fashion. He kept this up for a good sixty seconds, staring me as if he were trying to decide whether to fire me, or ask me to marry his spinster daughter. By the time he finished tapping, I would have welcomed either.

"I need your help with something, Jack," he said finally. "We have a new client; a big one. I gave them to Phil last Monday, but after a week he had nothing worthwhile to show me. It was all garbage."

Two things there didn't surprise me; one, that he'd given the job first to his little kiss-ass pet weasel,

Phil. Second, that Phil wasn't able to do anything with it, since Phil was an idiot. Strickland had never figured that out, or simply ignored it because he enjoyed the sensation of Phil's nose wedged firmly between his cheeks.

"Do you think *you're* up to the task?" asked Mr. Strickland.

I had no idea, but that wasn't the sort of thing you told your boss. You were always up to the task, even if you didn't have the slightest idea what the hell the task was. "Absolutely," I said, with my fiercest wishy-washy conviction.

"Good man," said Mr. Strickland. He opened a drawer and pulled a file out, then slid it across the desk towards me. "Ace it, and there might even be a promotion in it for you."

I was almost afraid to open the folder; anything that might warrant a promotion from the man who hated me so much had to be hellaciously difficult. But I picked it up and opened it anyway. I should have known better; my heart immediately sank down into my stomach when I saw what was inside. *"Crap!"* I thought, so loudly I was sure he must have heard me. I should have been watching where I was I going, because I'd just fallen into the deep end of the pool, a pool filled with-

"English Petroleum," Strickland said. "EP. Their stocks are down since the spill, and they've been hiring PR firms across the U.S. to improve their image on a local level. This is a *big* client. Bigger than anyone you've dealt with so far. And obviously you'd have your work cut out for you."

This I didn't want. I'm not on Greenpeace's speed dial for donations, but like so many people I was more than a little p.o.'d by what had happened down in the gulf. And now I was being asked to man a broom to help sweep it under the carpet.

"So what do you say, Danielson?" said Mr. Strickland. "Are you ready for the big leagues?"

I weighed the pros and cons. Pros, kiss up to Strickland and take the job, work my magic and make EP new and shiny, and maybe get that promotion and more money. Then I could fire Phil, get a Cadillac Escalade, make Brittany and her Daddy happy, have some sex. The cons, some nasty looks from a few fish at the Mall Of America aquarium, and a healthy dose of self loathing for helping everyone forgive English Petroleum for being negligent bastards and causing one of the biggest environmental disasters in Earth's history. The fish I could handle, but the latter...

"I...don't...know," I said finally.

My boss scowled at me. "What's there to know?" he asked grumpily.

I didn't think Strickland would understand or appreciate my moral conundrum, since he'd have to have morals himself to begin with. Instead I simply said, "I'd just like some time to think about it."

Mr. Strickland snorted. "Fine. But I want to know after lunch; someone's got to get on this. And don't let me down, Danielson. You need this."

I wasn't sure and didn't want to know what he meant by my needing this, but it was obvious our love-in was over. I put the file back on his desk and got up and walked out of the office.

I was going to need some help on this one. I'd never developed a taste for hiney, and wasn't sure I wanted to now; so far my dignity was battered but still in tact. Luckily Marty, my best friend and one person I could count on, worked right there at Image Makers. I was sure he'd understand my doubts and steer me in the right direction.

After all, if your best friend didn't have your dignity's back, who did?

"Kiss the booty," said Marty, taking a sip of freshly overpriced Starbucks.

It appeared my dignity was on its own.

"That's your advice?" I said, leaning back against Marty's cubicle wall.

"Yep. Smooch that sucker; again and again. Buy some Chapstick if you have to," said Marty.

"I prefer Carmex," I said.

"Anything that keeps your lips moist and ready to pucker," said Marty.

"So no chance for a speech about my principals?" I asked.

"Nope. Get in there and tell Mr. Strickland you love him, and you'll be glad to lower yourself to new found depths," said Marty. "If you were so worried about your principals you should never have gotten into PR in the first place."

I thought about bringing up my guidance counselor and shifting some of the blame onto her, but decided now wasn't the time. "I haven't seen *you* schmoozing him lately," I pointed out.

"That's because it wouldn't do me any good; we both know I suck at this. You're the one with the talent," said Marty. "Look, Jack, you've been working here for what, seven years now?"

"Nine," I said.

"Wow. Okay, nine," said Marty. "My point is, it's probably time to start playing the game by their rules, because you're not scoring many points your way. Grovel at the boss's feet and you'll win the big money."

"You mean, rip off those clingy last shreds of self respect?" I said.

"Yep. Just do it really fast, like tearing off a Band-aid," said Marty. "It's your only choice, really. Or have you forgotten about Brittany?"

"Not yet," I said. "But what does she have to do with it?"

"A woman like her, she's not going to wait around forever maxing out your gold card..." said Marty.

"All signs to the contrary," I said.

"...she's going to want an upgrade to platinum, eventually," said Marty.

"So what you're saying is?" I said.

"Either be a second rate American citizen for the rest of your life, or tell your morals to get stuffed and wallow in the muck with the rest of the successful capitalist pigs," said Marty. "And by the way, your morals will get over it when they're riding shotgun to work with you in a new Beemer."

"Escalade," I said.

"Same difference," said Marty.

I sighed, but had to admit Marty was right. The choice was simple, and I was making a bigger deal out of it than I should, which is something I did on a regular basis. It was probably time to grow up. I decided to tell Mr. Strickland I'd take the job and get on with this life thing. Maybe I'd bring Marty on board too; we usually worked well together. He kept me going in the right direction while I came up with all the ideas and helped him keep his job.

I didn't feel great about my decision but I thought I could live with it. Yeah, the fish were going to hate me but what did they know about life on dry land? There was a lot more to worry about up here than swimming around chasing after shiny pieces of metal.

On the other hand, they did seem to have a tendency to eat one another.

Maybe they'd understand after all.

Chapter 3:
"The death of an unpopular publicist."

My commute home was highlighted by hypothetical ads running through my head, featuring happy families driving automobiles fueled with EP gas. Unfortunately whenever the people got to where they were going, be it a beach by the lake or a cabin in the woods, they found it was now the habitat of hundreds of picket sign carrying, angrily barking, oil coated sea lions. I wasn't sure what the sea lions thought they were doing in my commercials; I was pretty sure there were none to be found in the gulf, so it really wasn't their fight, this time at least. But my brain seemed to have made them the unofficial mascot of all offended wildlife down there.

It had become immediately and unsurprisingly clear I wasn't going to enjoy my new task, but that sometimes went with the turf. Working in PR was a lot like being a lawyer. You weren't always going to like your client, be they scumbag criminal or scumbag corporation, but it was your job to use all your skills to present them in the best possible light. In English Petroleum's case I wasn't trying to make them appear innocent; I knew that was a lost cause. What I was shooting for was guilty with a good excuse, something akin to, "*Sorry for the mess down there, but ya know, without us, you'd all be walking to work."* And after spending the afternoon and half my drive home thinking about it more thoroughly, even that had degraded itself down to a simple, *"Oops!"*

The snow was still falling as I weaved my way through rush hour traffic; it was fast becoming one of those Minnesota storm days when you wonder if it's ever going to stop, or if you were going to be buried alive. The temperature had warmed up just enough in the early part of the afternoon to melt some of the slush on the roads but now had fallen again, and patches of ice were developing on the freeway. That was something I should have been paying closer attention to. But my head was too cluttered with sea lions to concentrate on anything but how to appease their fuzzy butts and Joe and Jill consumer, and both at the same time. The human mind can only process so much information, and mine was way past overload.

Surprisingly though, I can still recall most of what happened next. It was probably the sort of heightened awareness we find ourselves in when thrust into emergency situations (such as ripping out the crotch of your pants ten minutes into your first prom). I remember I was developing a splitting headache, and thinking that if I didn't get the promotion after putting myself through all this I was going to....well, be really ticked off, anyway. I had the stereo turned on; music usually helped me think, but it probably wasn't the brightest idea tuning in to Margaritaville Radio on the XM dial. I'd been hoping it would help ward off my ever encroaching wintertime blues, but all those sun, sand, and surf songs couldn't have subliminally been doing much for EP's Gulf defiling case.

I remember changing lanes and passing a slow moving Buick (is there any other kind?) and crossing into the middle lane. I felt my Suburban's tires slip a bit, but they caught the pavement again almost immediately. My mind was meanwhile wandering around, trying to come up with some angle for my campaign I hadn't thought of. I looked up the embankment I was whizzing past and saw an EP station, sitting there looking all innocent. I watched it go by in a daze, and by the time I looked back at the road, yet another slow moving Buick was smack dab in front of me.

I have no idea where he had come from; maybe he'd changed lanes and cut in front of me, maybe not. It didn't really matter; it was my fault. I should have been watching where the hell I was going. There was only one thing I could do now, and it was one of those things you should never do on slippery roads; stomp hard on your brakes.

My vehicle immediately confirmed this rule, and I began to fishtail like mad. I barely had any control at all and I was sure I was still going to hit the slower car in front of me, but by some miracle I slid around it and into the right hand lane. This would have been a good thing, but my slide also turned me fully sideways, my passenger door leading the way down the freeway. It gave me a rather unique view of the road, and I found myself watching traffic zip by through my windshield, which might be why I didn't see the off-ramp I was whooshing towards.

Remember those big, yellow, water-filled trashcan like things people are always crashing into in action movies? Well, there were none of those. There was, however, a nice, sturdy, metal railing separating the main freeway and the off-ramp, and my passenger door rammed into this with a not-so-wonderful jolt. My memory gets a little fuzzy at this point, and I'm guessing it's because I bonked my head hard on the driver's side window. I do remember coming to a very abrupt halt, and being grateful for being stopped and still in one piece. That is, until I spotted the semi truck barreling down on me.

I'm not positive if he'd been heading towards the off ramp or down the slow lane. All I know is he was now heading right towards me, trailer sliding sideways behind him as he tried to stop. I recall thinking how big he was and how much it was going to hurt when he hit me, and that was about it. My life didn't flash before my eyes, which I suppose might have been a good sign, in spite of my situation. Instead all that happened was I heard a loud, almost deafening noise, and felt a hard jolt, and everything went from wintery white to nothingness black.

Chapter 4:
"My head hurts, my cars trashed, but I'm not with Jesus."

I woke up surprisingly undead, and I don't mean vampire-like; that probably would have been an improvement on my condition. Instead my whole body felt like I'd been run over by a Mack truck, which was odd since I vividly remembered the word *"Peterbilt"* bearing down on me.

I was lying in a hospital bed, inside what I cleverly deduced to be a hospital; it was either that or a very clean and drab Red Roof Inn. I didn't have any tubes or expensively beeping machines attached to me, which I took to be a good sign, unless I was terminal and they'd already given up on me.

Marty was asleep in a chair next to my bed. I tried to sit up but immediately felt woozy, and flopped back down with an audible *"Ugh."* Marty opened his eyes; apparently he'd just been resting them. "Hey buddy," he said. "How are you feeling?"

I carefully and with some difficulty propped myself up on an elbow. "Do you remember that time I fell down the basement stairs carrying that keg at Gary's bachelor party?" I said.

"Yeah," said Marty.

"This is worse," I said, and laid back down again.

"Ouch," said Marty.

"So how did *you* end up here?" I asked.

"The hospital phoned me; they checked your cell. I guess they called Brittany first, but she told them I'd be closer," said Marty.

"That's my loving, caring girl," I said. I tried to sit up again and lasted about twice as long this time before I collapsed.

"Here," said Marty, and he grabbed the *raise the bed/nurse I have to pee* remote and propped me up until the ceiling no longer filled my immediate view. "Better?"

"Yeah, thanks," I said. "So what happened? I mean, why aren't we having this conversation in the morgue? I would have sworn that semi was going to squish me."

"I talked to the officer waiting to take your statement. The truck driver told him that at the last second his tires found pavement and he was able to turn a bit and avoid hitting you dead on. Instead he just nailed your front quarter panel and spun you around hard. You got *really* lucky," said Marty.

"I'll say," I said. "And my Suburban?"

"Not so lucky, I'm afraid. The same cop showed me a picture; it looked like a Picasso painting of an SUV," said Marty.

"So much for my ride," I said.

"How did it happen, anyway? You weren't watching Avatar on your phone again, were you?" asked Marty.

"No, I learned my lesson on that," I said. "I don't know what happened this time; well, yes, I do. I was distracted; by work, mostly. I just wasn't paying enough attention to what I was doing."

"It sounds like you're damned lucky to be alive, and at the very least lucky you weren't hurt a lot worse than you were. The doc said you can go home whenever you feel up to it. Evidently you've already been subjected to every expensive scan they have around here and you're fine, just a little battered and bruised," said Marty.

"Then I suppose I should try and get upright," I said, about to push myself into a full sitting position.

"Naw. Let me go get that cop first to take your statement. Maybe he'll be more sympathetic if you're lying there looking half-dead," said Marty, and he stood up and went out into the hallway.

I laid there in bed waiting, and when Marty didn't immediately reappear I got bored and began reliving the crash over and over again in my mind. At the time it had seemed like a run of the mill, car out of control, sliding down the road sort of occurrence; nothing that unusual. I'd been in a couple of accidents before, and you don't have time to be truly scared. It usually happens so fast the most you can do is think, "*Crap!*" and hang on for dear life. This time was no different. Yes, I was startled. And when I saw the semi I was more than a little concerned. But that was about it.

There was something about the whole thing that bothered me though, and I couldn't put my finger on what it was. It was like waking up from a dream. I felt there was something I couldn't quite remember, something that had happened during the accident that was important. But I had no idea what it could be.

It took Marty a while to find the officer, and by the time they came back I had whittled my mental dilemma down to three semi-hard facts. One, I'd almost died today. Two, something about it was bugging the hell out of me. And three, even though two seemed like a perfectly normal reaction to one, in this case it felt like anything but.

Which was why I had Marty take me to a hotel instead of my condo after I gave my statement. In my current state of whatever the hell was wrong with me I didn't want to just walk into my place, say, "*Hi*" to Brittany, watch some TV, and go to bed. I felt like something had to run its course. That and I was pissed off at my main squeeze for not coming to see me in the hospital.

I needed to do some soul searching, to try and come up with an explanation for my state of mind. I needed to be alone for a while.

I needed the Ramada Inn.

Chapter 5:
"Thank God the mini-bar is open."

Hotel mini-bars are dangerous things, especially for people like me who didn't want to leave their room. I checked mine and found it had everything I could need, then went out into the hallway and began the safari to find the ice machine. If you weren't planning on using it it was always right next to your room making racket all night, but if you did by chance need some ice it was usually off somewhere near Zanzibar. Eventually I found my prey, and after making the trek back to my room to get the bucket I had forgotten to bring with me, was able to load up on ice and lock myself back in my sanctuary.

I mixed myself a Captain Coke, then sat down and tried to relax. It didn't take long for the alcohol to start taking affect, which may have had something to do with the lovely pain killers I'd received at the hospital. Three drinks later and the two drugs were doing an amazingly hypnotic dance in my system, putting me into a state of utter tranquility I hadn't felt for quite some time. I felt pretty damned good, and even momentarily forgot why I was in a hotel instead of my condo in the first place.

There was a sliding glass door that opened onto a balcony outside my room, and I decided to go out and take a look. I was on the third floor, and the view I had over the wintery courtyard and a small sliver of downtown Minneapolis wasn't half bad. I brushed a few of inches of snow off a chair and sat down to enjoy it, the icy plastic seat sending my buttocks a wake up call.

The storm was finally tapering off, but enough flakes were still in the air to make for a beautiful evening. A cold, soft breeze was blowing and it felt good against my skin. It was quiet, the snow taking the sharp edges off the sounds of the city. I felt alone, but not lonely; the one doesn't necessarily follow the other, and I was like a hermit on a distant mountaintop seeking clarity; a hermit with spiced rum in his hand.

I took another sip of my companion, then stuck my drink in the snow on the table next to me. I was tired. Not sleepy tired, more like my body never wanted to move again tired. But I still felt better than I had all day. I was sitting on a hotel balcony in the snow, rum and prescription drugs swirling around in my system. I wasn't thinking about English Petroleum or any other work related bullshit. I wasn't thinking about Brittany and our dysfunctional relationship. And I wasn't at Wong's eating raw fish with her parents like I was supposed to be, listening to them bitch about liberals. Life was good, if only for the moment.

My eyes felt compelled to close and I let them, tilting my head way back, letting the last icy snowflakes of the storm alight on my face. Everything was right with the world, and I smiled.

And began to cry.

Not tears streaming down my face like I was watching *Rudy* again, just good and choked up. I'd had sensations like this before. I recall being on Gull Lake in northern Minnesota with my father; I was up visiting the family, one of the few times I'd managed to tear myself away from work and the Cities. It was amazingly warm for an early summers day, though the air still had a wonderful spring crispness to it. And though it was afternoon it was calm as midnight, the lake a mirror reflecting an incredibly blue sky. Green pines and birches covered the banks of the shore as we floated along, just talking and drinking ice cold beer.

I remember the stereo being between songs, the pontoon turning, and the sun hitting the water just right, sending a streak of gold towards our boat. And at that moment Etta James began singing, *"At Last."*

And just like now, I had started to cry.

It was the perfection of the moment that had caused it; the fresh air, the blue of the lake, cold beer, and Etta James. And being in that moment with my Dad.

As I sat there now all dewy-eyed and reflective, it occurred to me perhaps why these moments always hit me so strongly. The closest word I could use to describe it is shock. If you take an ice cold glass and thrust it into red hot water, there's a chance it's going to crack; that was me. My existence was so drab and dull that when I found anything close to a perfect moment, the contrast between it and the rest of my life was almost overwhelming. So although it was wonderful to be able to find and appreciate these rare little gems in time, the real problem was how I evidently felt about the rest of my life.

Suddenly I could also remember the last few lost seconds of the accident, as if one good realization deserved another. I could recall every little detail, even what I was thinking right before I blacked out; I had thought I was going to die. And in what I perceived to be my last moment of life, if I would have had a comic book thought bubble sketched above my head, it would have simply read, *"Oh, well."*

That was it? The plug was about to be pulled on the production titled Jack Danielson and the best closing line I could come up with was, *"Oh, well"*? The more I thought about it, the more it pissed me off. What the hell was wrong with me? Yeah, my life wasn't perfect. Who's was? That's no excuse for not being at least a little irritated mine was about to come to an end.

I stood up, brushed off the snow that had gathered on me, and went back inside. I poured myself another drink, not about to go all the way back out to get the one I'd just callously abandoned, and took a good long gulp from it.

In spite of a stretch over the last few hours that would have sent a mood ring into a tizzy, I'd never considered myself to be an emotional person. Something had to be done about my present state of mind, and maybe about my whole damned life, in case I did something stupid again like I just had and brought the whole thing to sudden close. The last thing I wanted was to end up dying all crabby, since it would *be* the last thing. But for the moment there wasn't a lot I could do to improve my situation.

It was time to sit down and talk to me, while my ghost was near.

Chapter 6:
"The me I can't explain."

Over the next few days I spent my time thinking, drinking, stewing and sleeping, in various orders and combinations. I didn't accept phone calls or visits from the maid, and I didn't watch TV; I just rumbled around my hotel room making a mess of it and me, trying to figure out when and where I'd gone wrong with myself and what to do about it.

My biggest problem, as far as I could tell anyway, was that I wasn't very happy with me. My second biggest problem was trying to define what exactly that meant. What made me who I was? My feelings? My career? My love life? My unhealthy fascination with pizza? There are things you can easily change in your life, and things that are much more difficult. If I didn't like me, the real me down at the core, could I change the bugger? If not, then *that* was going to be my biggest problem.

I tried a logical approach to the problem; that was me too, Spock's long lost ancestor on his mother's side (and he thought he got it from his dad). Analyzing was one of my favorite pastimes; just give me some data and I'd be content to curl up with it for hours, no matter how unhealthy dwelling on whatever it was might be. In this case I decided it was all about my chronology.

So I looked back over my time line to see if I could find any moments that had shaped me into who I was now. I'd been a normal enough kid, happily exercising the hell out of my imagination pretending to be a pirate, cowboy, soldier, cop, spaceman or wizard, depending on what genre of movie or TV show had excited me lately. When I moved on to junior high school that didn't change much, except I imagined my adventures in my head most of the time, since it was so important to act cool on the outside now that girls had suddenly appeared out of nowhere. They'd been there all along, of course, these softer, curvier little things, but I didn't know what they were for so I hadn't taken much notice of them. And during those junior high years I never did quite gain the knowledge I wanted about their exact usage, despite the fact that my best friend's parents had both *HBO* and *Showtime* and were gone a lot. But along with the use of a shoplifted and dogeared Playboy as a technical manual, I never stopped trying to work it all out.

When I got to high school it was all about music and cars, and yes, those same girl creatures. It was also about not getting haircuts and not doing what my parents told me, or at the very least, bitching about it first. In other words, I was a pretty typical teenager.

But I got decent grades and managed to stay out of any of the more advanced forms of trouble, and was happy and having a good time. Especially one lovely, warm, Minnesota evening when the music, car, and girl all came together, and I found out in the sweaty front seat of my Ford Pinto exactly what it was I'd been missing all that time.

And coincidentally discovered during the same night that I needed to get a bigger car.

Then it was off to college. As I've said before, I only had a vague idea of what I was supposed to be doing there. But for the first three years at least I managed to accomplish several important things; one, I learned how to drink. The dabbling I'd done in the trade during high school was strictly amateur stuff compared to the professional level of imbibing I participated in during my freshman, sophomore, and whatever you want to call that middle year of the five years I and so many others took to get a four year education. I hadn't yet declared a major, but if I had, it would have been in carousing.

College also broadened my horizons; I actually value that now more than the education itself. I met a wide spectrum of people from all over the country, and a few from around the world. I know taking general eds like anthropology and bowling are supposed to round you out as a person, but I think meeting different types of people and learning to get along with them is far more useful. That is, if you *do* learn to get along with them. There's always the chance you'll come out of school the same jackass ass you were when you went in.

By the way, one thing college won't do for you by itself is make you smarter; even if you learn what year the Peloponnesian war started or where your flexor digitorum is located, there's no guarantee of instant brains. If a cow managed to get a college education it would still be as dumb as a post; she would just be able to get a job easier than all the uneducated cows. It's what you do with the knowledge you gain throughout your life that gradually turns you into an intelligent person. And if you really apply yourself, maybe even a wise one. I'm nowhere near the latter; in fact, I'm way behind on becoming intelligent. But at least I know where I stand, and that's a step in the right direction. Hopefully I've still got time for a come from behind win.

But back to school, or me at it, anyway. As I said, I was whooping it up and genuinely enjoying the whole college experience while managing to still get a few good grades in the process. I even learned to pour drinks while working part time at one of the college bars near campus, which is still the best money per work exertion unit of any job I've ever held. I didn't in any way, shape, or form have my future figured out, however, but it didn't bother me because I was having way too much fun to care. That is, until *she* came along.

Yes, there was a woman to blame, and the one at this point in my life was Wendy. God, she was beautiful. And sexy. And smart, at least as far as I could tell without actually talking to her. All in all, she was the kind of woman a guy like me had absolutely no chance of getting unless he suddenly became famous, filthy rich, or saved the world with a bunch of Transformers. But I wanted her anyway, and badly.

It only took three months of pining for me to get up the nerve to speak to her; that and half a bottle of Jaegermeister. It was at a frat house party, and she was standing across the room in one of those short little skirts of hers that I was surprised weren't regulated by the federal government. My libido took one look and decided it was time for plunder, but as usual my wuss of a brain said her ship was more than we could handle. Cutlasses were drawn and a brief skirmish broke out, and when the smoke cleared, my mutinous sex drive and his co-conspirator, sailor's mate Jaegermeister, were at last in charge of the ship.

I took one more shot for courage, then sailed boldly across the room and right up alongside her. I managed to get her attention by clearing my throat about three times, and when she turned those deadly green eyes on me, stammered out some slurred confession of my undying love for her. Or lust. Or probably both. I don't remember precisely what came out of my mouth, only that it utterly failed to impress her in any way close to what I had imagined while meticulously planning out the moment for the last ninety days of my life.

I retreated back to my corner, my hull riddled with cannonball holes from her harsh rejection. I downed the other half of my bottle, went outside, and found an unlucky tree to lean on while I returned Herr Jaegermeister to Mother Earth where he belonged. Then I went back to my dorm room to pass out.

The next morning I replayed the whole affair in my head, over-analyzing it to death as always, and decided it was time to get my shit together whether it liked it or not. Never mind the fact that Wendy probably wouldn't have had anything to do with me even if I had been a stone cold sober law student instead of a Jaeg soaked third year with no clue what he wanted to be when he grew up. I would work out my future and fly right, and the next time a chance that I didn't have to begin with to get a girl like Wendy came up, I would at least have something to offer her besides licorice breath.

So come Monday I walked into my guidance counselor's office and told her I needed guidance, and the rest was history. I could see now that from that day forward I'd been a different person. A hard working person. And because I over-reacted and spread this new-found responsibility over all facets of my life, a very, very, boring person. All because Wendy didn't want to have sex with me. Maybe not the worst reason in the world to change your life, but the fact remained I didn't care for the results.

Having worked all that out, the only thing left for me to do as I sat in my hotel was to decide how the hell to do something about it. I didn't have a lot of resources at my disposal. Heck, I didn't even have my laptop with me, so I couldn't look up the answer on Wikipedia. I was totally on my own, and almost helpless without my trusty computer.

All I had was a hotel room and a bunch of alcohol, and that probably wasn't going to be enough. But that didn't mean I wasn't willing to try and pull a MacGyver and find a solution using only what I had at hand to work with. Though it would have helped if the mini-bar had been stocked with duct tape.

Luckily for me I got some help from a guardian pheathered angel I didn't even know I had.

Chapter 7:
"Jimmy Dream."

I woke to a severe pounding in my head, this one even worse than my hospitalized one. It was a particularly noisy pounding, and it took me a moment to realize someone was banging on my hotel room door to the rhythm in my noggin.

I swore and pulled myself out of bed, threw on my by now trusty hotel robe, and went over and opened the door.

And was surprised to find Jimmy Buffett standing in the hallway holding a pizza. I stood staring at him, my mouth hanging open, wondering what on earth could have brought him to Minnesota and my door, and thinking how chilly he must have been walking around in those shorts.

"Well, are you gonna invite me in?" he asked in a friendly tone. "The pizza's gonna get cold."

"Yes! Yes, come in, Jimmy," I said. "Can I call you Jimmy?"

Jimmy strolled inside, his flip-flops making that wonderful flop-flip sound I had forgotten all about as he walked across the carpet. "That's my name, isn't it?" he said. He looked around the room at all the clutter and mess. "Where can I put this?" he asked, holding up the pizza.

I hurried over and knocked my coke can and mini liquor bottle sculpture off the table, and Jimmy put the pizza box down and opened it. The smell of pepperoni immediately wafted through the room, obliterating even the beer and dirty socks smell that had had the run of the place.

Jimmy looked on, bemused, as I stared longingly at the pizza. "You look hungry," he said. "Go on, grab a piece; that's why I brought it."

"Thanks," I said, reaching into the box and pulling out a big slice. "I am starving." I took a huge bite, and was rewarded by the explosion of cheese, sauce, flour, herbs, and spices that make pizza the numero uno super power in my gustatory world.

Jimmy stood watching me, a little smile on his face. "Good?" he asked.

"Um," I said, around a second mouthful of the food of the gods. "Delicious."

"That's great," he said. He took a slice for himself, and the two of us stood there munching out on Jimmy's pizza until it was gone.

When we were finally finished, I said "Thanks, I needed that."

"Yeah, I know," said Jimmy. "Ya gotta eat when you're whooping it up, or you're liable to toss out your anchor."

"I'll remember that," I said. "Can I get *you* anything, Jimmy? A rum and coke or something?"

"No thanks, I'm good," he said.

"Then can I ask what you're doing here?" I said. "Not that I mind, of course. I'm just a little surprised to see you."

"I came to talk to you of course, son!" said Jimmy. "Come have a seat."

I sat down in one of the chairs at the table and Jimmy did the same, putting his feet up on the bed.

"What did you want to talk to me about?" I asked.

"Why, your problem, what else?" said Jimmy.

"Really? You think you can help me?" I said.

"I might be able to point you in the right direction, but you'd have to do the rest yourself," said Jimmy. "So what seems to be the predicament?"

I sighed, trying to figure out how to put it into words. "I just feel lost."

"You're not lost; you're right here," said Jimmy. "Figuring that out would be a good start."

"It's like I don't know who I am," I said. "Or at the very least, I don't *like* who I am. I'm not sure where this guy who has control of my body came from, but I've decided I don't care for him very much; he's kind of an asshole."

"It's your body," said Jimmy. "Tell him to get the hell out!"

"I would, but then what?" I asked. "Who do I move in instead?"

"You, of course!" said Jimmy.

"But who is that? Like I just told you, I don't know who..." I said, trailing off.

Jimmy smiled one of those big smiles of his. "Son, you're making this way too complicated," he said. "This is *your* life, and no one else's. All you have to do is get out there and live it before it's too late."

I sat thinking for a moment, then said, "And what if it's too late already?" I asked.

Jimmy stood up, then leaned down and put his hand on my shoulder. "Trust me; it's never too late."

"But you just *told me* to get out there before it's too late," I pointed out.

"Never mind me; I'm just a dream. Just do as I say," said Jimmy.

"Even if you keep contradicting yourself?" I said.

"Well, since technically this is all in your subconscious, you're the one contradicting yourself," said Jimmy. "But it's clear you obviously have something you're trying to tell yourself. Just pick out the good bits and run with them."

I thought about what he had said, then stood up. "You're right. Sitting here in this hotel room isn't going to do me any good. I don't have the slightest idea where I'm going, but I guess I better get underway," I said.

"That's the spirit," Jimmy said. "And, Jack, don't ever give up the search for who you are. There's no greater treasure than being yourself, and being someone else is the ultimate fool's gold."

I put out my hand and we shook. "Thanks for the advice," I said. "And for the pizza; I think they both helped. At least I know now who has to do something about the me."

"Just remember to relax, and to try and enjoy whatever you decide to do," said Jimmy. "Life isn't half as complicated if you don't spend all your time thinking it is."

I walked Jimmy to the door and he put on his aviators, then waved goodbye and disappeared down the hallway. Moments later I heard a plane engine start above me, and I rushed out onto my patio. I was pleased to find that it was sunny and warm outside, and the hotel now overlooked the ocean instead of snowy Minneapolis.

I heard a roar overhead and looked up, and the *Hemisphere Dancer* flew into view. She dipped her wings at me, and Jimmy waved out the window and shouted, "Take it easy!"

I waved back and decided to try and do just that.

Chapter 8:
"Don't know if I'll ever go home."

I woke to a severe pounding in my head, this one even worse than my hospitalized one. It was a particularly noisy pounding, and it took me a moment to realize someone was banging on my hotel room door to the rhythm in my noggin.

I swore and pulled myself out of bed, threw on my by now trusty hotel robe, and went over and opened the door.

And wasn't too surprised to find Marty outside. I grunted a greeting of a sort at him, then went back and collapsed face first into my pillow.

"Hello to you too," said Marty, as he came in and shut the door behind him. "Glad to see you're still alive, at least."

"That makes one of us," I said.

"Do you have any idea how many times I've tried to call?" said Marty.

"I stopped counting at four," I said. "That was when I unplugged the phone."

"And your cell?" asked Marty.

I pointed in the general direction of the balcony. "It's down in the courtyard somewhere; that happened after Brittany's ninth crabby text. I guess it couldn't live with itself any more."

"Well, you had us worried sick about you," said Marty.

"I doubt that. Brittany doesn't start vomiting until she hits a hundred and ten pounds," I said.

"Get up," said Marty.

"No. Do you have any idea how early it is?" I said.

"Do you have any idea how early it isn't?" said Marty.

I turned my head a bit and peeked at my closed curtains. It was daylight, I could tell that much at least. "Somewhere between seven and seven."

"It's five o'clock," said Marty. "PM."

"Like I said; early. Go away and come back in twenty-eight hours," I said.

"Do you even know what day it is?" asked Marty.

"None whatsoever," I said, not wanting to try and work it out.

"It's Thursday," said Marty.

"Hm; I would have guessed it was today," I said.

"Get up," repeated Marty.

"Yeah, like saying it twice is going to get me moving," I said.

"When's the last time you had something to eat?" asked Marty.

"Last night, actually; I still have the indigestion to prove it," I said. "There's still a couple slices left if you're interested."

"No thanks," said Marty. "Get up."

"That's three times. How do I unplug *you*?" I said.

"You can't. Get up and we'll go get something to eat," said Marty.

"I'm busy," I said, burrowing further still into my pillow.

"Yes, wallowing," said Marty. "For some reason."

"It's something to do," I said.

"So is drinking, by the looks of it," said Marty, eying my platoon of dead little airline soldiers that I'd strategically placed around the pizza box.

"Yes, but now that you mention it, I've run out. I was going to call the front desk and get restocked, but since you're here you could do me some real good and toddle off to the liquor store. I'm tired of numbing myself fifty milliliters at a time," I said.

"I don't toddle," said Marty. "But I'll make you a deal; you come out and have some real food, and the drinks are on me."

I pondered his offer for a moment then raised my head a bit. "Can we have margaritas?" I asked.

"Fine, yeah. We'll walk over to the Parrot," said Marty.

"Good," I said, and slowly dismounted off the bed. "I'm in the mood for margaritas for some reason." I grabbed my coat and pulled it on and headed towards the door.

"Um...pants?" said Marty.

I looked down. "Why?" I said.

"Just humor me. But first go into the bathroom and get cleaned up. You smell," said Marty.

"Of course I do. I have a nose, don't I?" I argued, standing my ground.

""No shower, no margaritas," said Marty.

"Geesh! You've got more rules than Brittany," I said, trudging off to the bathroom.

I finished my last forkful of chicken enchilada, and pushed the plate away from me.

"Feel better?" said Marty.

I suppose so," I admitted, reluctantly.

"So what's going on, anyway? Are you having some sort of nervous breakdown?" asked Marty.

"Nope. Nervous is the one bad thing I don't seem to be," I said.

"Then what's the problem? You missed three days of work and didn't even call. Strickland's about to have a seizure," said Marty.

"One can only hope," I said.

"Yeah, well, I can only cover for you for so long," said Marty.

"Then don't bother," I said, then picked up my margarita and took a drink.

"Well, can you at least tell me what's with you? Whether you believe it or not, Brittany is worried too, and I promised her I'd find out what was wrong," said Marty.

I looked around the Purple Parrot Bar at all the seemingly happy faces; everyone looked like they were having a good time. Everyone but me, that is.

"I don't know if you'll understand," I said. "Hell, I don't even understand."

"Try me," said Marty.

I scratched my head and sighed. "Okay, here goes; I've come to realize I don't have a clue who I am."

"Welcome to the club," said Marty, picking up his Corona and toasting me with it.

"I'm serious," I said.

"So am I. You think *I* know who *I* am? Or that anyone else in this room does? The rest of us are in the dark too," said Marty. "So get over yourself."

"If that's true, don't you think it's pretty sad?" I said.

"Maybe; I don't think about things like that. I just get up every day and do what I have to do," said Marty.

"That's another thing. I'm tired of every day being alike; nothing ever happens," I said.

"What do you mean? You were just in a very exciting car crash, weren't you?" said Marty.

"Alright, nothing *good* ever happens," I said. "It's the same every day. Go to work, do the job, drive home, get nagged, watch TV, go to bed. I see the same things, eat the same things, and do the same things, every single day. And no offense, talk to the same people."

"Exactly; it's called life," said Marty.

"Well, I don't want to do it anymore," I said. "And I'm not going to."

"Really," said Marty doubtfully and a pinch sarcastically. "Then what's your plan?"

I started to give an answer and realized I didn't have one, at least in that moment. But then I heard something in the background of all the restaurant noise that made my path became clear, or at least slightly more visible. "Listen," I said.

"You're going to listen? That sounds even more boring, and I bet the pays not so good, either," said Marty.

"No, listen," I said. "The song."

Marty listened. "Yeah? So?"

"It's Jimmy Buffett," I said.

"I know," said Marty. "What are the odds of *that* in a tropical themed restaurant?"

I'd forgotten all about the Jimmy dream I'd had last night, but it came rushing back to me now as I heard one of his songs playing. *"Changes in latitudes, changes in attitudes,"* I said.

"Fine. Like I said, I hear it," said Marty.

"Well, that's what I'm going to do," I said.

"You're going to go on vacation? Good, you could use it; you haven't taken one in years," said Marty.

"I'm not taking a vacation. Well, maybe I sort of am," I said. "A very extended one."

"Then what *are* you going to do?" said Marty.

I paused, wanting to put it in just the right words. "I'm gonna live my life like a Jimmy Buffett song," I finally said, dramatically.

Marty did a little spit take with his beer, then looked at me as if I'd said something crazy, which I suppose I had. "I think you need to go to another hospital and get a second opinion on that head bump of yours; Saint Mary's is just around the corner."

"I'm perfectly fine," I said, believing it. "In fact, I don't think I've ever been thinking so clearly my whole life. Look, I had this dream last night, about Jimmy Buffett, and-"

"Oh, god," groaned Marty.

"No, really; I think it was a sign," I said. "That I should change my life. Drastically."

"So let me get this straight; you think Jimmy Buffett came to you in a dream and told you he wants you to dress like a parrot, drink a lot of rum, and start a reggae band or something?" said Marty.

I thought about it. Did Jimmy Buffett come to me in a dream? Probably not. He's a busy man, what with the music and the bars and the books and the hotel. But who knows. "No, I don't think that. But I think *I* told me that, disguised as him."

"What do you plan on doing, then? I hope you realize that even Jimmy Buffett probably doesn't live his life like a Jimmy Buffett song," said Marty.

"Well, maybe not twenty-four seven," I said. "But I bet he comes pretty close most of the time."

"So which one?" said Marty.

"What do you mean?" I asked.

"Which song?" said Marty.

I considered that. "All of them, I guess," I said. "Except maybe that Elvis impersonator one."

"What's wrong with Elvis?" asked Marty, defensively.

"Sorry; I forgot he's your main man. At some point I'll grow some mutton and put on some weight, too, just for you," I said.

"That's better," said Marty. "But you can't be serious about this. I mean, what, are you going to quit your job, too?"

"Nope," I said.

"Good," said Marty, relieved. "Without you there it wouldn't take them long to figure out I have no idea what I'm doing."

"I'm just not going to go anymore," I said.

"And that's not quitting?" said Marty.

"Maybe it is. But why should I waste one more second of my life at Image Makers?" I said.

"Oh, I don't know. So you can tell Strickland where to stick it, maybe?" said Marty.

Perhaps I wasn't thinking so clearly after all. "Good point; I'll be in tomorrow for that. You know, I almost died Monday because I was too busy trying to come up with a way to make people feel better about English Petroleum to concentrate on driving. What a useless way to go that would have been. And why the hell should anyone cut them any slack? Do you have any idea how many lives they screwed up?"

"Humans or dolphins?" asked Marty.

"Both. EP should be nailed to the wall, and instead two years from now they'll be recording record profits again," I said. "But at least I can not help them do it."

"Okay. You hate your job and you're going to quit. No biggie, people do that all the time without going off the deep end," said Marty. "Then what?"

"Then I'm going to sell everything I own and take off," I said, my plan taking shape as we discussed it.

"Going down..." said Marty.

"I can't stay here; I need to get out and explore. I've only been out of Minnesota once, and that was for the PR convention in Omaha," I said.

"That was pretty exotic, wasn't it?" said Marty. "So what, you're just going to bum around, then?"

"For a while at least. And then, well, I don't know. But I'm sure something will come up," I said.

"And if it doesn't?" said Marty.

"I'll worry about that later," I said.

"But what if-" began Marty.

"I don't know!" I snapped. "Look, this isn't scientific; I don't have everything figured out yet. But that's the point! To just see what happens."

"Is that what you're going to do with Brittany, too? Just see what happens? Or are you planning on taking her along on this little voyage of self discovery of yours?" said Marty.

"Um...she sort of slipped my mind," I said, which she had. This was a problem. Brittany and me on the road together without a plan? Yeah, like that was going to work. Spontaneity wasn't exactly her strong suit; we'd have reservations in the finest hotels wherever we *wandered* to next. "I'll have to have a talk with her. You know Brit; there's no way she'd be up for something like this."

"An hour ago and I would have said the same thing about you," said Marty. "So you're just going to break up with her?"

"I guess so. We've been a mess for quite a while now anyway. I know she's not going to be pleased, but if she really cares about me she'll understand," I said.

"Well, you might want to sell everything you own first, *then* tell her, so she won't have anything to throw at you," suggested Marty. "Are you going to go home tonight, then?"

I thought about it. "No, I better spend one more night at the hotel planning my strategy. It's going to be a busy day tomorrow."

"Yeah, I'll say. Just don't show up at work until after I arrive. I want to be there when Strickland's head explodes," said Marty.

"I promise. You'll be there for the big bang," I said.

I was excited for the first time in years. For once I didn't have a clue what was coming next, and that was very liberating. It was a little scary too, of course. Routines, no matter how mundane, are comforting in a way. But I was breaking out of mine whether I liked it or not.

So far it felt damned fine.

Chapter 9:
"I'll never work in this business again."

"Danielson! Get your butt in my office!"

It was Friday morning, and I'd barely gotten my entire body inside the door when I heard his majesty's bellow; he was on his game today. But I was on mine too, so instead of obeying I went over to Marty's cubicle to chat.

"So how's it going?" I asked, casually.

"Fine, fine," said Marty. "I don't suppose you changed your mind overnight, did you? I'm going to miss having your work to hide behind."

I smiled a big smile and said, "Do I look like a man who's changed his mind?"

"No, you don't. In fact, you look far too happy for your own good. If I didn't have a wife and kids I'd consider drinking the purple Kool-Aid with you," said Marty. "What's in the satchel?" he added, pointing at the cheap art folder I'd picked up last night during my trip to the office supply store.

"Stuff," I said, patting it.

"What kind of stuff?" asked Marty. "It isn't the letter bomb kind of stuff, is it?"

"Hm; in a way, yes," I said.

The door to Strickland's office opened and he poked his head out and looked around until he spotted me. "Danielson! What are you, deaf? I told you to get your ass in here!" he hollered, then went back inside and closed the door again.

I smiled my new smile again and looked around the room. I was pleased by all the nervous looking faces of my colleagues peeking at me from their cubicles, obviously wondering what the hell I was up to.

"So are you going in or not?" asked Marty.

"Yes," I said.

"When?" asked Marty.

"When I'm sure he's fully irritated," I said.

"The suspense is killing me," said Marty. "That and he's going to start yelling at me next, since you're standing in my cubicle."

"Coward," I said.

"Yeah, well, I haven't gone totally insane in the last few days like some people I know," said Marty.

"Alright, I guess I don't want him taking you out too if he starts lobbing grenades. I'm sure he's good and riled up by now anyway," I said.

"Thanks. I don't need the refrigerator box I work in to become a war zone," said Marty.

I gave Marty a little salute and walked over to my soon to be ex-boss's door. I calmed myself a bit, then opened it and went inside. He was busy on the computer as usual, furiously typing away and feverishly ignoring me, so I went over to one of the chairs facing his desk and plopped down in it. He glanced up at this brazen behavior on my part, his brow scrunching down so low his nose was in danger of disappearing. Then he went back to clicking away on his keyboard.

I took out my new iPhone and started playing around with it while I sat there waiting. I knew buying it wasn't exactly in keeping with the Buffett lifestyle, but everybody's on the phone these days so I'd decided to make an exception. If I was going to sell off all my stuff I was going to need a replacement for my old deceased one anyway, so people could get a hold of me. And besides, the thing was way cool.

"Danielson!" said Mr. Strickland.

"Just a sec," I said, trying to pull up the internet and ignore Ronny at the same time. It took a minute but I figured it out, then satisfied, turned the phone off, and stuck it back in my pocket and looked up.

And was pleased with the lovely shade of pink my boss's face had obtained. "Are you finished?" he growled.

"Yes, I think so," I said.

"Good," said Mr. Strickland. He steadied himself, like a tuba player about to tuba, then bellowed, "Where the hell have you been?"

"Drunk in a hotel," I said, matter-of-factly.

"I don't want to hear any excu...did you just say you've been drunk in a hotel?" said Mr. Strickland.

"Yes, I did," I said.

Strickland looked me over, trying to figure out how to handle this honest piece of information I'd just given him. "Does this have anything to do with your accident?"

"I don't know. Maybe. Sort of. Who cares?" I said, nonchalantly.

Strickland shook his head as if to clear it. "Never mind. I hope you know you can't just not show up or call and continue to work here."

"Oh, absolutely," I said, agreeing one hundred percent.

"Good; don't let it happen again," said Mr. Strickland.

"I won't, I promise. *It will never ever happen again*," I said, emphasizing each word.

"I'll let it pass then, provided you get to work over this weekend on the EP campaign," said Mr. Strickland.

I picked my art folder up off the floor where it had been leaning against my chair, and put it in my lap and patted it. "I've been working on it already; got it right here."

Strickland looked suspicious. "I thought you said you've been drunk for the last few days."

"I was, but I quit at only *half-drunk* last night," I said. "Managed to come up with some pretty good stuff, too. It's a little rough around the edges, and I didn't get a chance to do the art on most of it, but I think you'll be pleased."

"Well, let's see it then," said Mr. Strickland.

I stood up, and went to the corner and grabbed the easel that Strickland kept in his office for just such presentations. I made sure the cards I had were in the right order, then placed them on the easel, the front one reading, *"EP: Your Earth Friendly Friend."*

"Are you ready?" I said.

"Yes, just get on with it," said Mr. Strickland, grumpily.

"Okay. This first one is good because it shows both English Petroleum's generosity and their product's affordability," I said.

"Alright," said Mr. Strickland, putting his arms on his desk and leaning forward in anticipation.

I removed the front card to reveal the one behind it, then read the caption I'd written last night, out loud; *"We're so crazy at English Petroleum, we're giving oil away! Come on down to your nearest Gulf beach and scoop some up!"*

Mr. Strickland stared at the card, not sure what to make of it.

"No?" I said. "How about this one then; it's short and to the point." I pulled the card aside and revealed the next, again reading the catchphrase aloud; *"Hey Gulfers; the check's in the mail!"*

"Look, Danielson..." began Strickland, sensing something was up.

"Still too long? How about this," I said, and showed him the next card; *"Oh, well; shit happens!"*

"Are you finished?" Mr. Strickland asked angrily.

"Nope, got two more," I said. I pulled the card aside, revealing my personal favorite; *"Hey, you Americans spilled our tea into the ocean; payback's a bitch, isn't it?"*

"You think you're pretty funny, don't you Danielson?" said Mr. Strickland, standing up.

"No, wait; I have to show you the last one, too," I said.

"I've seen quite enough," said Strickland, waggling a fat finger at me. "And let me tell you something-"

"No, let me tell *you* something!" I snapped, years of pent up angry of my own coming back at him. "Sit down, and shut the hell up!" He looked back at me, and for the first time I saw him for what he really was; a tired, scared, bully of a man who had nothing in his life but a job he probably didn't like any more than

71

I did mine. I watched him as he quietly sank back down into his big leather chair, and decided immediately not to show him the last card I'd worked so hard on; I didn't need it now.

"You know, you've been making my life here at Image Makers miserable for years even though I always did my job and was good at it," I said. "And I put up with it. And you know what? Now that I think about it, it's not your fault; it's mine. No one's been holding a gun to my head. I should have told you where you could shove it a long time ago and I didn't. But I'm telling you now; I don't need this bullshit anymore. I quit, Mr. Strickland."

Strickland looked as if he was about to say something, but stopped, maybe because he knew there wasn't any point. Or maybe, like any bully, he knew I wasn't afraid of him anymore, and that scared *him*. In any case, he just sat there watching as I gathered my cards together and put them in my folder, and walked out of his office for the last time.

When I entered the main office I went over to my cubicle to gather my things, but realized upon looking them over there was very little I wanted. I grabbed the framed picture of Brittany off the shelf; it didn't seem right, no matter what our future might be, to just leave it there. Then I grabbed my two best cubicle buddies and headed over to Marty.

"Here," I said, tossing my favorite toy to him. "You can have my stress piggy."

"What about her?" asked Marty, pointing.

"No way; you're not getting my hula girl," I said, holding up Maria. "She'll be traveling with me. Besides, you need stress pig more."

"So that was it in there? You quit?" said Marty.

"Yeah, I did," I said.

"Well, that was dull. I hardly heard anything," said Marty. "Where was all the shouting?"

"A lot of it was close-captioned; here," I said, handing him the satchel. "Those should give you some idea."

Marty thumbed through the cards, chuckling a bit from time to time. "Nice. I especially like the drawing of Strickland kissing *your* ass. I bet he enjoyed that one too."

"I didn't show it to him," I said.

"What? Heck, you should have taken *Victory* down off his wall and put that up instead," said Marty.

"I know. I thought that summed up what I wanted to say, but I was wrong," I said. "It hasn't been him all this time; it's been me."

Marty shook his head. "If you say so. But I could have sworn he was the one riding your ass and not the other way around," he said. "So what's next for the new Jack Danielson?"

I sighed. "Well, now I have to go home and talk to Brittany. That's not going to be nearly as much fun as this was. I'm not looking forward to hurting her."

"Yeah, that's probably going to be rough," said Marty. "Give me a call later if you need to go out and have a drink or two afterwards and unwind."

I screwed up my face. "Um, thanks, but I'm pretty liquored out right now; it doesn't even sound remotely enjoyable. But swing by over the weekend. I'll let you have first dibs on a condo full of *my life so far.*"

"I'll bring Katie," said Marty. "She has better taste than me. And control of the budget."

I looked around the office I'd so grown to hate over the years. All those little cubicles dividing us up like livestock. The florescent lights hanging above, sucking the life out of everyone. The stuffy, unnatural, recycled air. I'd always felt trapped here, though I knew now I hadn't been. It was like the door had always been open, but I hadn't evolved enough to have the opposable thumbs to turn the knob and escape. But I had 'em now.

I stuck one of my hands and its newly grown digit out to Marty.

"Hey, we're going to see each other again," said Marty. "You just told me to come by your place, remember?"

"Yeah, but not as co-workers," I said.

Marty nodded, then clasped my hand and shook it.

"Thanks for making this place almost remotely bearable," I said.

"Right back at ya," said Marty.

I took one more quick look around and walked out the door to freedom, my Maria by my side.

Chapter 10:
"She's going out of my condo."

I walked into my living room, and was smothered by a five foot-ten blonde who threw her arms around me.

"Jack! Thank god you're alright. I was so worried," Brittany said, squeezing me tightly. It felt mighty good; this was going to be even harder than I thought.

Then she released me, leaned back, and slapped me hard across the face. "Don't ever do that to me again! Do you know how long we waited for you? Daddy was furious!"

Or maybe not so hard after all.

"What do you mean, waited?" I said. "Where were you? You didn't go to the restaurant, did you?"

"Well...yes. I thought you'd meet us there," said Brittany.

I looked at her as if to say *You've got to be kidding me.* "You've got to be kidding me," I said. "I'd just been injured in a major car wreck; which kind of sushi to order was the last thing on my mind."

"You always just get the number four," Brittany pointed out helpfully.

"That's because I can't tell them apart!" I said, then sighed. "Look; I don't want to fight."

"Neither do I. Why don't we go have lunch instead and you can make it up to me," said Brittany, reaching for her purse.

"I don't want to do that, either," I said, although I had to admit I was feeling a bit peckish.

"Well what *do* you want?" Brittany asked, using her exasperated with me voice.

"I want to talk. Sit down," I said.

"Fine," said Brittany, plopping down snottily on the couch, which wasn't an easy thing to do, but she had the gift. "So what do you want to talk about?"

I tried to decide where to begin. I was going to go back to Christmas of ninety-one when I didn't get the guitar I wanted, but figured she wouldn't find it pertinent, and it would take all day for me to get to my point. Which would have made it a perfect way to stall, of course.

"I've been thinking things over the last few days. My life, everything," I said. "I'm not happy."

She looked at me irritably. "Jack, don't you think you're a little young to be having a mid-life crisis?"

"Hey, if that truck would have hit me a few feet to the right I'd be having an afterlife crisis right now, so I think I'm entitled," I said.

"So, what did you come up with with all this *thinking* of yours?" she asked, obviously annoyed I would engage in such a distasteful activity.

"You're not going to like it," I said.

"I already don't like it, and I'm getting hungry," she said. "Just tell me what's going on so we can get things back to normal."

"That's the point; I don't want to get things back to normal," I said. "I want to get things to a state of serious abnormality, at least for me."

"What the hell are you talking about, Jack, and what does it have to do with us and lunch?" said Brittany.

"Well, now that you mention *us*..." I said.

"What about *us*?" she demanded. I didn't answer, being a coward and all that. Then I saw what looked like a thought creep across her pretty little face. "Wait a minute; are you breaking up with me?" she asked.

Just what I'd been hoping for, that she'd say it first so I wouldn't have to. "Yes, I am. But if it makes you feel any better, it's more of a by-product of changing everything *else* in my life."

She sat there staring at me from the expensive sofa I'd bought for her to park her perky bottom on; the one with the little white flowers I hated so much (the ones on the couch, not on her bottom). "So you're telling me it's over? Just like that?"

"I'm afraid so. You've got to admit we've been going nowhere for some time now. I am sorry it had to happen like this, but not as sorry as we'd both be if we kept this up for much longer," I said. "And the same would be true if I hadn't quit my job today."

"You quit your job, too?" said Brittany. "Jack, shouldn't we have talked about that, first?"

"Don't take your eyes off the ball when we're so close to the goal line, Brit," I said. "I just broke up with you, so I don't think you have a say in my career anymore."

"You've gone crazy, haven't you?" said Brittany. "I bet you're getting that male menopause thing early."

"Why is it because I want to do something different from the boring ass existence I've been living that everyone assumes I've gone nuts?" I said. "Maybe it's the rest of you who *don't* do it who are bonkers."

"Fine. Do what you want then. But if we're through, I want the dining room set," said Brittany.

"Why on Earth would I give you my furniture?" I said.

"Because I picked it out," said Brittany.

"You picked *everything* out!" I said. "But I paid for it."

"Well, I just want the table and chairs," she said. "And the bedspread."

"Too bad; you're not getting them," I said. "I may have paid you to be my girlfriend, but I refuse to pay you not to be. You can have everything in your closet. Technically your clothes are all mine too, but if it will make this any easier..."

Brittany stood up in a huff, a semi-natural state for her. "Just wait till Daddy hears about this, then we'll see. I'll be back for my things," she said, then whirled in yet another huff and headed for the door.

"Uh, key?" I said.

Brittany whirled around again, this time extra huffily. She dug her keys out of her purse and took my condo one off her key ring and tossed it at what I assume was my head, since it flew off into the kitchen (spoiled girls can't throw). Then she whirled in one last huff and stomped out of the building.

Looking back I know I probably could have handled the whole thing better. Brittany didn't really deserve my ill-executed breakup, and we had had some good times together. I didn't have the knack for the relationship thing, so I didn't have the knack for gracefully ending one either. But it was over at least.

And by the way, she did get the table and chairs eventually. And the bedspread.

And the sofa with the little flowers I hated so much.

And, yes, I am a wuss.

Chapter 11:
"I used to have stuff one time."

The next few weeks went by like a blur. I took out ads in both Twin Cities papers, and put listings on Craigslist and eBay. I contacted consignment stores and put up garage sale signs. I worked almost as hard as when I was working, and having people parade through my condo daily was more than a little bit irritating. But it was worth it in the end.

It was odd and a little painful watching my belongings go out the door, mostly in the hands of complete strangers. Our things give us comfort, and they're a sign that shows us we're getting somewhere in life; at least that's our perception. But they can also serve as an anchor, and as each possession disappeared I felt more and more liberated. It would be a pain in the ass to keep moving with a waterbed, for example, unless it was installed in the back of a circa nineteen-eighties custom van with a beach mural airbrushed on the side. By the time I was done playing Sears and Roebucks I was planning on being a lean, mean, ready to travel machine.

One of my toughest decisions had been whether or not to buy a new vehicle. On the one hand I planned to do a fair amount of flying since there were no roads going to the Caribbean yet, except for the Keys. So renting a car one way from place to place seemed to make more sense than driving one I owned. In the end though, I bought an old, beat-up, Cadillac convertible, red with a white top. It meant I'd have to fly back to whatever airport I had previously flown out of, but the thought of blasting down the highway in an old rag top, music blaring, was too appealing. Besides, I finally got the Cadillac I'd always wanted, even if it had more rust on it than my fun side.

The day eventually came when everything I wanted to part with was either sold or donated to the Salvation Army. Marty was going to store a couple of boxes of my personal stuff in his attic until when and if I had a place again of my own to keep it. My condo was still up for sale, but even with the economy in the crapper it was bound to sell sooner or later at the ridiculously and realtor disapproved low price I had put it at. I could now fit everything I owned in the trunk of my car, except for my car, of course. All but one thing, that is.

"Are you sure about this?" said Marty, looking at that one thing.

"Yes," I said, looking at it too.

"Because you don't seem so sure to me," said Marty.

"I said I'm sure," I said.

"I mean, I've seen sure, and you sure don't look sure," said Marty.

"Just take it," I said.

"Okay, as long as you're sure," said Marty.

"I am sure," I said.

Marty looked at it again. "I could store it for you if you like, until you need it again."

"Would you just shut up and grab an end?" I said, taking a position next to my fifty-two inch, top of the line, high definition, love of my life, LCD TV.

Marty took a spot on the other end. "You know, I bet Jimmy Buffett has one twice this size," said Marty.

"Yeah, and I bet he doesn't cart it off to Africa with him when he travels," I said.

"You're going to Africa?" said Marty.

"No, I'm not ready to be chased by angry rhinos quite yet. I thought I'd start with testy iguanas first and work my way up the food chain," I said. "Lift."

We carried the TV out the front door and put it carefully in the back of Marty's GMC.

"Big; it barely fits," said Marty, now having that glow that I'd had when I'd first brought the thing home.

"Yes it is; thanks for reminding me," I said, gazing at it longingly. "I wish I had a shrink ray right about now."

Marty closed the gate of his truck, and my prized possession and I were officially parted. Then he got out his wallet and handed me five one hundred dollar bills. I felt cheap and dirty, like I'd just sold my wife into slavery.

"So when do you leave?" asked Marty.

"Early tomorrow," I said. "Don't have much choice, really; I'm out of furniture."

"Then I guess this is goodbye, amigo," said Marty.

"For now at least. I'll be in touch on Facebook," I said.

"Not quite ready to be totally disconnected from society yet, are we?" said Marty.

"No, I'm not. Besides, I want to be able to rub it in to everyone how much fun I'm having," I said.

"Couldn't you just go old school and send a postcard?" asked Marty.

"You can't attach a digital photo to a postcard of a bikini clad island girl coming out of the ocean all wet and glistening," I said.

"True. And if you could the mailman would just swipe it anyway," said Marty.

We finally ran out of things to blather and stall about. It was odd; Marty was one item on my checklist I hadn't really considered when contemplating all this. But now that it came down to it, there was no escaping the fact that I was going to miss him, and a lot more than I had thought. But that's how it is with your best friends; they are so steadfast in your life that you tend to take them for granted, right up until the point when they're gone.

Marty and I shook hands as coolly as two clumsy white dudes were able to, then we gave each other a manly hug.

"Take care, bro," said Marty.

"You too. And take care of my TV," I said.

"I will. Have a Mojito for me when you get to paradise," said Marty.

"I'll do that," I said. I watched him get in his truck and drive away, firing off a couple of goodbye honks as he went.

And that was that. It was time for this astronaut to go into quarantine and order one last pizza from the House before bedding down for a not so good night's rest on the living room floor in his sleeping bag; the final countdown to liftoff had begun.

My last thought before drifting off to sleep that night was, *"Exactly what the hell is a Mojito, anyway?"*

Chapter 12:
"If I could just get it on hard drive."

The next morning I pulled out my laptop and fired it up. Mr. Spock said, *"Good morning, Captain"* and I opened up my word program and began to type.

Today was the day I officially begin writing all this stuff down more or less as it happens; it was Brittany's father's idea, of all people. When they came by to get her things he told me I should begin keeping notes; a journal of sorts. He didn't say why and I didn't ask; we weren't exactly close, my hating him and all that. But when I thought about it later, it seemed like a good idea even if he had come up with it. I figured maybe someday someone else might want to read about whatever adventures I did or didn't have, the same way I liked listening to Jimmy's songs. So I took the time to go back and type out what had led me to this point and promised myself to keep it updated, provided it didn't get in the way of any of my fun.

So here I was or am now, depending on when or how you look at it, pressing on keys as words formed on the screen. And I realized the second I typed something I was doing, it was in the past. It's like a joke I heard once from the late, great, Mitch Hedberg. It goes something like this; *"Would you like to see a picture of me when I was younger? No, because every picture of you is you when you were younger."* It's the same thing with writing. If you type *"I'm writing this now"* and hand it to someone to read, by the time they do so it isn't true anymore. So really every non-fiction book that tells a story should be put in the history section.

Why am I pointing all this out and what the hell does it have to do with my story? Nothing, really. I'm probably boring you with it because I'm nervous, and I'm stalling yet again, which is a huge part of my defensive skill set. When I close this laptop I'll walk out the front door and get in my rocket ship and blast off to go and explore the cosmos. That in itself isn't what makes me nervous; it's what I've done to get ready to do it, all the parts of my life I've tossed aside to prepare for this insane mission. I suppose it's like your wedding day. You really shouldn't be that nervous; you made the decision to marry the person you're standing next to months ago. But on the big day it's real at last, and I guess that's where I am too, or was when I wrote this.

But enough is enough. I want to do this, and now is always a better time to do something you want to do than later, because later you might not be able to do it anymore. I'm going to end this now before I type something I'm going to regret, even more than what

I've already written. So, goodbye for now, Houston.
This is astronaut Jack Danielson, signing off.

See you on the sunny side of the moon.

Chapter 13:
"The Cedar Rapids run."

I ended up getting a much later start on my odyssey than I would have liked; I stopped to say a quick goodbye to my parents, which turned out to be anything but, of course. So by the time lift-off officially came it was right into some sort of high school/college hockey/basketball tournament traffic, which did little to keep me in the happy-skippy-giddy frame of mind I'd started the day out in. But aside from a smattering of farewell cuss words tossed at a few well deserving Twin Cities drivers, I persevered and finally broke free of the metro area traffic snare.

Spring still hadn't fully sprung, so the rag top was firmly up in place as I whizzed down the highway. But I had a supply of Nacho Cheese Doritos, peanut M&Ms, and a Buffett compilation MP3 CD in the stereo, so I was loaded for bear otherwise. And best of all, I had my Maria shaking her hula thang on my dashboard to keep me company.

Overall, my financial plans for falling off the radar had gone pretty well. I'd made a healthy enough profit on the difference between the insurance money I received for my almost paid off Suburban, and the purring like a kitten but looking like a chewed up tomcat red Cadillac I was rolling in now. When I added that to the cash for my house full of Ikea, and the nest egg I'd squirreled away in spite of Brit's ever growing shoe collection, I knew I could safely screw around for some time; and I hadn't even sold my condo yet.

I had a general but vague idea of where I wanted to go, and what I wanted to see to start out with. It was by no means etched in stone however, and I'd tried to leave a little wiggle room for spontaneity. But I did have one destination vividly marked on my agenda in permanent ink; I'd even picked up some walleye beads, the state fish of Minnesota, to throw to the lovely ladies. Well, trout beads, anyway, since they were the closest I could find, but would the southern belles down on Bourbon Street know the difference? There weren't likely to be too many female Babe Winkelman wannabees shaking there ta-tas off the balconies, so I figured I wouldn't be arrested for attempted ichthyological fraud. The city of New Orleans was calling, and I wasn't going to miss my chance to finally see the Big Easy I'd heard and dreamed so much about.

It seemed fitting anyway to plan a landing in the unofficial capital of the gulf. The whole EP car crash thing had been more or less the catalyst for my escape from the ordinary, and I was more than happy to go down and leave some tourist dollars in New Orleans;

even *if* the Saints had stopped my Vikings one inch away from the Super Bowl. Besides, if I crossed off every city or state with a team that ever had a hand in slapping a Minnesota one down, I probably would have had to stick entirely to the Caribbean. And only then if the Negril Spliffs hadn't knocked the North Stars out of Stanley Cup contention when I wasn't looking.

Luckily for me and the foreign part of my travel plans, I already had a valid passport. I'd applied for it during the great Brittany marriage scare of last spring; not so I'd be ready to flee the country, though the thought had crossed my mind once or twice. But to be ready to distract my other half with a surprise vacation someplace tropical. The threat eventually went away and the trip never happened, but the passport remained, ready to whisk me off to semi-exotic locations.

Such as somewhere not in Iowa. Just as the sun sank beneath the farm filled horizon, I finally came to a big, happy sign welcoming me to Minnesota's more pig friendly southern neighbor's neighborhood. I rolled down the window to check out my new climes, but was a little disappointed to find it didn't seem all that different, other than the aroma of the freshly fertilized field I happened to be passing at the time. It was exciting never the less; it was a new state, and it showed I was making progress and getting farther and farther away from my natural habitat. I was like some bass-ackwards bird flying south for the spring, except I didn't have any intention of migrating back north when winter came.

I continued on as the night grew deeper, making good time since it was past the farmer's bedtimes. I'd been on the open road only a few hours, yet I'd already doubled the number of states I'd ever been in besides Minnesota. Not exactly a million miles from the nest, but I was at least putting a little distance away from cold hard fact and heading towards hot and fanciful fantasy. And, for better or for worse, all this being in the middle of nowhere gave me space and time to think.

I remembered what Marty had asked me the night I'd come up with this course of insanity I'd set my ship upon; what Jimmy Buffett song was I trying to live my life like? Tunes like *One Particular Harbor* and *Tin Cup Chalice* sprang immediately to mind, but neither of those or any others I could think of exactly fit what was going through my head. So the better and bigger question was, what had my me meant when he'd said he wanted to live his life like a Jimmy Buffett song?

After a few more miles of contemplation I still didn't know for sure, but decided that maybe what I was really trying to do was find my own song. Or to rewrite the one I already had, depending on your philosophy about such things. And that perhaps Jimmy's tunes were just good inspirations to help me pen my own. I could live on things that excite me, waste away a little now and then, hear Mother Ocean's call, and end up dying while I'm living instead of living while I'm dead. I could pick and borrow, live and sing, the Jimmy lines I liked the best, and then add a few of my own verses and hope the whole thing harmonized to my satisfaction. And that years from now it would become a golden oldie, a melody that I'd never grown tired of playing. That was my goal; to concoct my own lifesong gumbo, something tasty and tuneful, easy on the palette and the ears. And good for my soul.

I pushed on for a couple more hours, and when I came to the next big city, pulled into a Motel Six and called it a driving day. My eyes were growing weary, and were beginning to spend more time closed than open, not a good state for them to be in if I wanted to avoid another close encounter with one of the many semis that were trucking around me in the night. Other than needing to be at the New Orleans airport four days from now I wasn't on any kind of a schedule anyway, so the only hurry I was experiencing was that of being spurred on by my own anticipation for a taste of something different. But that would have to wait until the next manana.

Today had only been a day of beginnings, but every journey, story, or song needed one of those, too. I had my start out of the way now, and had a vague idea of what it was I was searching for, here away from my every day; a song I could be happy to call my own.

Not a bad opening verse for a simple Cedar Rapids run.

Chapter 14:
"I was thinking today about Elvis."

I almost managed to crash the Caddy today. I'd send out a big apology to all the drivers I've yelled at for being stupid over the years, other than the fact that it's an American tradition to get pissed off at people for doing something you're at least as guilty of as they are, and I'm a firm believer in traditions.

I blame Marty anyway (see, it's always someone else's fault). There I was, driving along minding my own business, zooming past Memphis, when suddenly a sign popped up to tell me that Graceland was another thing I was also zooming past. I knew Marty would never forgive me if I didn't stop and pick him up a cheap Taiwanese souvenir of an American icon, so I tapped the brakes and cut over quickly to try and catch the Elvis exit, and just about ran an old VW bug off the road in the process. The driver displayed a well deserved finger to me, but I managed to get off the highway and down into one of the birthplaces of rock and roll.

I didn't know that at the time, though. I was just making a short, spur of the moment pilgrimage for a friend. I dutifully followed the signs to the Memphis Mecca, and pulled into the parking lot of Elvis' home and signed myself up for the platinum tour.

I have mixed feelings about the whole thing. On the down side, I immediately wondered if Elvis had charged eight dollars just for parking at his house. I admit it would be a great way to make some extra money off your friends, that is if you still had any afterwards. Especially after hitting them up for an even bigger chunk of change to come inside and check out your pad. The whole thing was kind of weird, walking through this tacky, yet strangely appealing monument to rock and roll excess, and knowing that the King himself had sat in that chair or passed out on that tiled floor. All in all I'm not really sure it was worth it, but I did find a t-shirt in the gift shop that I thought would placate Marty.

I have to say up front that I, myself, wasn't a huge fan of Elvis. Oh, I liked him. He was Elvis, for crying out loud. But I had a hard time connecting with this chubby guy in a white, sequined jumpsuit, singing the *Impossible Dream* on a Vegas stage; not past the point of enjoying its kitschy Americana, anyway.

But then I went down the road and took the Sun Studios tour.

Ya gotta love movies; at least I do. They give me more good information then any other source at my disposal. In this case it was *Walk The Line,* the movie about Johnny Cash. As I came out of Graceland, feeling a bit disappointed about the whole thing, I spotted a shuttle bus going to Sun Studios. Again, me in Memphis with no idea why I should care I was there. But I remembered the scene where Johnny comes across the studio and eventually cuts a record, and that it was Sun Studios where Elvis got his start, too. I decided what the hell, I'd already spent good margarita money on the King, might as well waste some more. So I jumped on board, figuring I could at least avoid more parking fees that way.

But it was hardly a waste. To me, Sun Studios is the flip side of Elvis, the good side. The real, raw, king of rock and roll. The tour was inexpensive and parking was free, which I appreciated even if I didn't have a car with me. And Sun was what mattered about the man. It's like a football game and ESPN. You watch the game on Sunday and that's what a football player is, or at least the only part I care about. They're all out there on the field, putting everything they have into winning (well, most of them are anyway). Then you turn on ESPN, and ninety percent of what they babble about is something negative, like which player sent what reporter dirty pictures, who got the DWI, and who wants a fatter contract. I'm sorry, but that's not football. What happened during the three hours on Sunday was football.

Elvis was Elvis because of his music, what he did in the studio and on the stage. Graceland may be part of the man, but to me it's the depressing side of the man. It's the place where he lost who he was, in other words his music, and it eventually I think killed him. What made him Elvis was done in places like Sun Studios. *Especially* Sun Studios, as I found out when I picked up a CD of those first recordings. There's nothing like good, stripped down, no bullshit rock and roll. There's no way I can describe it; you can't really do music justice by talking about it. You'll just have to check it out for yourself sometime; maybe then you'll see the real Elvis too, if you haven't already.

After the tour I wandered up and down Beale Street and suddenly found myself smack dab in the middle of the blues, or at least a very gaudy version of them. Music clubs intermingled with tacky gift shops, and there were a few dark, seedy bars like like B.B. Kings place that I would have loved to have just hunkered down in and let my foot stomp along to some killer blues. But I would have been cutting into my New Orleans time if I did, and though it was tempting, I knew that Memphis wasn't going anywhere. So I took the time to buy a pair of fuzzy dice to hang from my rear view mirror, then headed off towards my final destination in the town I had had no intention of stopping in before today.

It was a bit of a walk, and my car was getting farther and farther away. But eventually I turned a corner, and there it was; the Lorraine Motel where Dr. Martin Luther King Jr. had been assassinated, now the National Civil Rights Museum. It was one of the most eerie experiences of my life, almost like time traveling; it looked like nothing about the place had changed. And there was the balcony itself where America had hit one of the lowest points in its existence.

I walked up as close as I could and just stood there. It felt like something was different, something tangible in the air. It was as if I could perceive ripples of effect going away from the spot, like a large stone of change had been dropped there in the water. I don't know if that makes any sense, but I can't describe it any other way. It was an important place, and whether the area emanated that or my mind simply knew it and was telling me so didn't matter.

I didn't go through the museum. Maybe someday I will, but the balcony alone spoke volumes to me and I wanted to leave it at that. Instead I walked back to Sun Studios and took the shuttle to Graceland and my car, and drove off towards Jackson and my eventual stop for the night.

Memphis is a cool city; it's fitting that it's the home of the blues and the birthplace of rock and roll. It's old yet vibrant, and sad yet exuberant. When you consider what happened after the death of Dr. King and if you believe that music changes our lives, it's dizzying to think what the world and especially America would be like if you took Memphis out of the fabric of time. I guess we'd still be back in the forties, listening to Perry Como and sleeping in twin beds; and doing god knows what to one another.

Thank you, Elvis, Jerry Lee, Johnny, B.B. and the Howlin' Wolf.

And thank you, Martin.

Chapter 15:
"Crayola."

Today, the box of crayons that colored my world grew a little larger.

I arrived in New Orleans during the morning, just as I'd planned. Driving into the city was a remarkable experience in itself; yes, most of it looked like any other city, but just going to a place I'd heard about my entire life was a great thing, and knowing what the city had been through with Katrina and seeing it alive again gave me a warm, fuzzy feeling. It showed me again what amazing things we humans can do when we work together; it's a shame we do it so infrequently and often need a disaster to make us all unite.

I was staying right in the French Quarter; it cost me a little more to have a place in the heart of the action, but I didn't care. Being able to walk out the door and into the beating heart of the city was more than worth it. I got settled in, then went out and wandered the worn, narrow, cobblestone streets.

My mouth would have been happy to just hang open in awe at the surroundings my eyes were seeing. I've always had a thing for pirates; not *that* sort of thing, although Miss Elizabeth and Angelica were damned appealing. But just the whole pirate milieu in general. And the streets of New Orleans looked to me like they belonged in a pirate town, which is where they were, of course. I could imagine horse drawn coaches replacing the cars; that's all it would have taken, really. And since a few such buggies went by now and then, it made said imagining all the easier.

The proper buccaneer type buildings were already in place, a mixture of French, Spanish and Creole architecture (I took a tour the next day in one of those horse drawn coaches and knowledged up). It was just too pirates of the Caribbean for someone brought up on strip malls and log cabin homes to not get me excited. And out of the corner of my eye, whenever I flexed my imagination, I swear I could see a scurvy band of scallywags carousing on one of the wrought iron balconies over my head. Arrrrrrrr!

One of the things that surprised me (besides all the pirates) was the weather; it was nice, but I'd expected it to be warmer. I guess I had this movie induced image in my head of it always being very hot down in the south, with everyone constantly walking around bathed in sweat. But it would only get up to a moderate seventy degrees that first day, though a bit humid. I wasn't complaining, mind you. It was still close to freezing up in Minnesota, and I was getting the same thrill now as I did when I skipped school once and spent the day at the arcade; it felt like I was being naughty, and naughty was nice.

I stopped walking on a particularly interesting old corner and leaned back against the brick wall of the bar behind me, so I was out of pedestrian traffic. I closed my eyes; they'd already had the bulk of my brain's attention, and it was time for my other senses to move to center stage. I relaxed my mind and breathed in deeply the smells and sounds of the soul of New Orleans.

It was almost like coming out of a coma; the rush of color to my brain was almost overwhelming. Spices and musical notes intertwined, emanating from the open doorways along the street. My nose twitched, ready to happily lead me like a good bird dog to any number of places my mouth would be happy to go. And the sounds; there is simply something different about live music, and I don't mean recorded live music. When you hear it in person it mixes better in your ears, like it was meant to be heard on the spot where it was being played. It just sounds more...alive. I guess that's why they call it live music.

I reopened my eyes, not sure now where to begin with so many delicious auditory and gustatory choices, so I strolled up and down Bourbon Street for a while to get the lay of the land. On the music side I had my choice between Jazz, Blues, and either Cajun,

Zydeco or Creole, depending on what I decided to call whatever I was hearing at that moment, since I didn't have a clue what the difference was between them. Of course there was good old rock and roll, too, but I'd heard that before on many an occasion, and wanted a taste of something different. And the food; it simply wasn't fair putting all those flavors in front of a Minnesota boy who thought Buffalo chicken was the end all of the seasoned world.

Eventually my stomach won the wrestling match with my ears for immediate attention, and I ducked into a small joint claiming to have the best Gumbo in the world. As Forrest would say, now I don't know about that. But after my first mouthful I knew that if I spent the rest of my days trying to find out whether or not they were exaggerating, my life wouldn't be a wasted one.

Shrimp. Onions. Celery. Tomatoes. Bell Peppers. Spices. Nothing that exotic; so why the hell did it taste so bloody good? All I knew was that I'd had to choose between Creole Gumbo and Cajun Gumbo, and that my waiter wouldn't tell me which one was better; only that they were different. It gave me far too many options for my own good. I could eat Cajun Gumbo while listening to Cajun music, and Creole Gumbo while listening to Creole music. Or I could get really wild and eat Cajun Gumbo while listening to

Creole music, or vice-a-verse. Good thing I didn't know at the time there was also Zydeco Gumbo to go with Zydeco music, or I would have probably passed out at all the possibilities.

And I wish someone would tell me exactly what it is about great atmosphere that makes food and drink taste better, and what makes great atmosphere great to begin with. I've been in some very fancy restaurants, dragged there by Brittany, filled with mahogany, brass, and a truckload of ferns. Eh, nothing. But there I was in Raimond's, a collection of eclectic artwork half-haphazardly hung on the walls, sitting on a beat up wooden chair, at a beat up wooden table, placed on a beat up wooden floor, eating from a simple ceramic bowl filled with simple ingredients, and it couldn't have been more appealing if it sang to me. Which I think it did, just not on an auditory level. And the piece of french bread I used to wipe my bowl was indeed a welcome tool to not leave behind a drop.

After my lunch in heaven I wandered a bit, then walked into the one place I'd heard about before coming to New Orleans, *Pat O'Briens* (okay, I'd researched it on the net the night before). I made my way through the gathering afternoon crowd into the main bar, and grabbed a stool just as someone got up to leave. I knew I had to be a good turista and have one of Pat's world famous Hurricanes, and after ordering and receiving one, sat back and checked out my surroundings.

I turned my back to the bar while I sipped my drink; partially because they had big mirrors on the wall and I didn't feel like staring at myself, but mostly because I wanted to be able to watch people. I felt a little out of place; everyone seemed to be having a good time with one another, and I was on my own.

Most of the room had that distinctive French Quarter feel to it, replete with black ironwork. But the ceiling was covered with big, ceramic, German beer steins, which were an odd contrast to the rest of the atmosphere. And they also made for an odd little coincidence when Otto sat down next to me while I stared up at them, and struck up a conversation.

Like the beer steins, Otto was also from Germany. And just like them, Otto was also big, about six foot five and broad shouldered. He looked like he should have been standing on a mountaintop wearing Lederhosen and a little hat with a pheasant feather in it, chopping down innocent fir trees while belting out *Ein Prosit* at the top of his lungs. It was also entirely possible that Otto wasn't from Germany at all, but just enjoyed pretending he was. He claimed to be from Hamburg, and that was as believable a German city to be from as any I guess, since it wasn't like I could question him about it; if he'd said he was from the third moon of Saturn I wouldn't have known any less about the place. But one minute Otto's accent would be there, thick and heavy like a good bratwurst, and the next it would be totally gone as if it had just stepped out to look for some sauerkraut to go with itself. It didn't matter, though. I liked him immediately, and anyway, you don't question big guys about their nationality who you can picture happily swinging axes.

Otto had become separated from his friends, but he didn't seem to mind; he struck me as the kind of guy who was going to have a genuinely good time no matter what happened. "Ve be drinkenen some beer today, ya?" he was saying to me yet again, a half hour into our conversation.

"Ya," I said, clinking glasses with him for the fifth time already.

"So, this is your first time to New Orleans, isn't it?" Otto asked.

"Yes, it is. How could you tell?" I said.

"Turn around and look at yourself in the mirror," said Otto.

I did, and saw that stranger I didn't know staring back at me again. "Okay, I'm looking," I said.

"Do you see someone who looks like they are in one of the biggest party places in the vorld?" asked Otto.

He was right; the guy I saw could have been in church, suffering through a really boring sermon. "No, I don't," I admitted to him.

"New Orleans is a place to relax, and to get crazy and cut loose," said Otto. "You look like you don't know vhat to do, like you're trying to figure everything out."

That was the wrong thing to say to me, or at least the wrong way to say it. "That's because I *don't* know what to do and I *am* trying to figure everything out," I said. Then I spent the next hour telling him all about my life and what had brought me out on the road and down to New Orleans. In very great and lengthy detail. In other words, for sixty minutes, I was the guy or gal you wish you hadn't sat down next to on the plane, or made eye contact with at a party.

To his credit, Otto didn't suddenly get up to pee and never come back. In fact, I don't remember him having to pee at all, now that I think about it; maybe that was a sign of German superiority in engineering. Instead he listened intently, except for whenever a girl with nice *die brüste* happened to walk by. When I finally finished he put a big arm around my shoulder, then removed it and gave me a hearty slap on the back.

"You're in New Orleans, now; you'll see; every little thing is gonna be all right," he said. "Trust me."

I took that to mean shut up, stop vorrying, and relax, which seemed like good advice, and decided to give it a try. "So what do we do first, then?" I said.

"Ve be drinkenen some more beer," Otto said, taking a big swig from his.

"Ya, I know that part," I said. "Then what?"

"Then, ve go find the ladies and try to get gebumst werden," said Otto.

I wasn't sure if he meant we were going to *get bumped weird* or find *a weird bum, a*nd which kind of bum he might be talking about. "Meaning?" I said.

"Ve go get laid," he said.

That didn't sound too bad, although I'd never had the knack for finding spontaneous sex, which was part of the reason I had rented Brittany for so long. "I'll give it a shot," I said.

"Good to see you already have some beads," said Otto, checking out the twenty-four strings of trout beads encircling my neck. "You're ready for action."

"Yeah, but I have to find someone to throw them to soon or I'm going to end up walking hunched over for life; these things are heavy. Maybe ve should drinkenen our beers and head out into the street," I said, stealing Otto's line.

"Ya, good idea," he said, agreeing.

The day was still fairly young, but it was beginning to show promise. Yeah, the growing crowds were a little annoying, but they were fun too. It just depended on whether someone was bumping into me and spilling my drink again, or if I was being pushed against a lovely coed or three. I'd made a new friend who seemed like a decent guy who knew how to have a good time in the Big Easy, and stupid as it sounds, I was glad to have a mentor with that sort of thing since it never came easy for me.

Even a mentor who's name turned inside out was *Toot*.

Chapter 16:
"Yes, I was a pirate."

Down in the French Quarter they have what must be the best deals involving beads since Manhattan was purchased. Come to think about it, considering what they ended up with out east, New Orleans probably has the best bead deals, period.

There's an elegantly simple bartering process in place. People on balconies hold up beads and cheer at girls below; girls lift shirts revealing ta-tas, and people on balconies cheer louder and throw beads to girls. It reminded me of the stock market floors I'd seen in movies, the guys on the balconies shouting, *"Buy! Buy! Buy!"* and the gals down below yelling, *"Sell! Sell! Sell!"* It also reminded me of trying to get the family Cocker Spaniel, Gaby, to roll over, except the girls in New Orleans seemed far more cooperative when you offered them a treat.

I'd lost Otto somewhere between balcony number three and five, but that was okay. Even though we'd been having a good time together, it was actually easier to move through the throng by myself than to try and do so while keeping up with him. I was feeling no pain, except when someone stepped on my foot; flip-flops are not the best riot gear for braving party mobs. But I'd downed enough Hurricanes, Mint Julips, and

Pimm's Cups to be good and festive, and to not care.

My shirt was quite festive by now too, and that was yet another rookie mistake; don't wear white if you plan to decorate yourself with a percentage of each drink. Something loud and flowery will provide spill camouflage nicely, the more colors the better. Maybe that's why tropical shirts are so popular in all the party places.

I had absolutely no idea what time it was, other than late. I'd ditched my watch before leaving Minnesota (I could always cheat by looking at my phone anyway) having no desire to keep track of the hour. What difference did it make? My bank account was my only time piece. It didn't matter if it was three AM or PM; the only thing that might make me take notice of when or where I was would be if and when my funds started running low. Until then, any watch I wore should just say now.

And as for the now and what I was doing in it, New Orleans was turning out to be everything I'd thought it would be, and more. I'd thought I knew what I was in for, but you really can't imagine what it's going to be like to experience the revelry of Bourbon Street amidst the *vive la différence* that is New Orleans. I'm obviously far from a festivity expert, but I have spent the rare night bar hopping with Marty in downtown Minneapolis. And though I was doing basically the same thing in the Big Easy as I had been back in Minnie on those nights out, (looking at girls, enjoying an adult beverage, listening to music), the colorful kaleidoscope that was New Orleans's atmosphere turned it into something special. I guess where you do a thing is every bit as important as what thing you are doing.

I wandered down yet another lovely, bordering on seedy in just the right way French Quarter block, then came to an abrupt halt and stared. It sat there on the corner, this little structure out of time, and I wondered how I'd missed it before on the many times I'd already walked up and down Bourbon Street. Perhaps it only materialized at night; a building not haunted by ghosts, but a building that was a ghost itself. Or maybe the light had to be at the proper level of dimness for it to appear, as if it wouldn't allow broad daylight to ruin its ambiance.

Whatever the reason for its absence on my previous meanderings past the spot, it was there now; *Lafitte's Blacksmith Shop Bar.* It was just a small place, made of old stone and wood, looking like the most ancient building I'd ever seen in my life. And as I stood there gazing at it as if I was looking into the past, I could hear it whispering to my inner pirate, beckoning me to it like a siren of the sea.

114

I walked towards it, anxious to be inside, while hoping it would live up to its outward appearance. I couldn't tell for sure what I was in for, since though I strained my eyes to see through the open doorway, I could see little; the interior was very dimly lit, and I could only make out a few dark shapes. But as it turned out that dark would be perfect for dark business, and my final step past the old open door, a scratched and beaten, wooden and wrought iron thing, felt like a step back into the age of piracy.

Of course, there were no pirates to be found, at least not unless you were looking hard enough. I got a beer at the bar and sat down in a shadowy corner and peered over it as I sipped, and let my imagination free from its leash to run around. Then I began to make them out; a scattering of crusty looking scallywags, skulking about amidst the tourists and locals. I watched a couple of fights break out between them, then let my eyes follow a buxom, raven haired serving wench as she made her way through the crowd. Eventually she stopped and handed a pewter tankard of rum to Captain Jean Lafitte himself, who stood by the fireplace in the center of the room, planning some skullduggery with a fellow privateer.

I sat in my corner for the rest of the evening, abandoning the bright lights and thrills of the rest of Bourbon Street in favor of my imaginings. I just couldn't help myself; it may not have been as much fun for everyone, but just sitting there in the dark, soaking up the atmosphere and playing pirate for the night, put a big ol' smile on my inner buccaneer. I found out the next day Lafitte's was considered to be the oldest building in America that was being used as a bar. Something I could now cross off my bucket list, if only I had one.

I didn't go back to Lafitte's after that first evening; you should never return to the scene of a crime, and anyway, I doubt if it would have been the same. Instead I went back to the normal (if anything one does in New Orleans could be called entirely normal) bar hopping, food sampling, and music dancing I'd begun before being shanghaied into Lafitte's crew. I had a great time, and would love to go back one day and do it all again, but what I'll truly never forget is my little, dusky corner of the Quarter.

Yes, I was a pirate, and right on time.

Chapter 17:
"Defiling gravity."

Winston Churchill once said, "Democracy is the worst form of government, except for all those other forms that have been tried from time to time."

I say, "Flying via commercial airlines is the worst form of travel, except for all those other forms that have been tried from time to time."

I'd only flown one other time in my life, on that notoriously boring business trip to Omaha, and I'd forgotten how much I hated and loved it. And though I was amazed on my flight to Mexico to find it had managed to get even worse, I still had to love it. Or at the very least, no matter how many indignities I suffered, how willing I'd be to put up with it and do it again the next time.

I was irritated to discover that one of the first steps in planning your trip now is making the monumental decision of whether to pay to have the airline allow your luggage on board, or if you want to "carry on" a smaller version of all your stuff for free. The airlines seemed to have started this shortly after September 11th, when airport security began to be amped up. I'm not sure how having a hundred and fifty bags full of who knows what within arms reach of the passengers makes flying safer now, but I'll let that one pass.

I know it makes getting on and off the plane a helluva lot more fun, and there's nothing quite like having a sweaty, smelly armpit in your face as some guy tries to wrestle his oversized bag into the overhead bin. And I'm sure the new security measures have done amazing things for the ziplock baggie industry, not to mention for whichever high tech company out there shrinks all the toothpaste, shaving cream, and mouthwash down to an allowable size.

If it really makes us safer, then I guess I'm all for it, but it seems like just another way to throw common sense out the window. I know they don't want larger bottles of toiletries that might contain explosives on board, but I reckon a baggie chock full of a bunch of *little* bottles of explosives would do a fair amount of damage, too. And it seems like preventing a tourist from bringing a Key Lime pie onto the plane is taking us into a new level of wackiness, unless the guy is also wearing clown shoes and a big red nose, sure signs he plans to push it into the pilot's face and make us crash.

Personally, the only reason I would even consider blowing up a plane would be the lack of legroom; I'm not close to NBA power forward height, but I still had to cram myself into my seat, and pretty much stay in one position for three hours. If an announcement had come over the PA that we'd been diverted and I was going to have to suffer for another hour or two, the prospect of ending it all right then and there with a big boom would have had a fair amount of sex appeal. Give all the passengers another inch or two, hand us a five dollar Subway sandwich instead of a bag of peanuts, and I guarantee the odds of any on board violence will go down tenfold.

But in the end, no matter how early you had to get up that morning, no matter how rude the Delta or American representative was, no matter how many times you put your shoes and belt back on, and how many times the beverage cart smacked into your limbs, there's still nothing like that moment when you finally, touch back down on Mother Earth. You're a thousand miles or more from where you began, and if you're lucky, you're reasonably on time and it's still daylight. And if you're even more lucky, the bags you decided to pay to come with you underneath actually did so, and you're ready to begin your vacation.

Not exactly beam me up Scotty, quick, but it sure beats the hell out of driving for three days.

Chapter 18:
"Why don't we get pissed."

I was on my third Corona before the wheels of the bus hit the Hyatt parking lot, delighted to find the shuttle in Cancun had a cooler full of ice cold beers on board. You know you're on vacation when they start selling you drinks while you're still en route to the hotel.

I'd sampled my first taste of tropical heat when I walked out of the airport, and it made my beer taste all that much better now. It felt different from the warmest days in Minnesota, and the closest thing I could compare it to was opening a clothes dryer; just a blast of hot air that left me with little doubt I wasn't up in Kansas anymore.

Another clue to my new whereabouts was the huge, blue, wet horizon I was staring at through the bus window. I hadn't made it down to the ocean while I was in New Orleans; there were too many shiny things distracting me. And I'd managed to miss it from the plane as well as we flew over it today, sitting in my aisle coach ticket seat, while contemplating my life as a sardine. But I was seeing it now, and it was one of the most beautiful sights my eyes had ever taken in.

I don't know if we love water so much because we come from it, or that sixty percent of our bodies are made of the stuff. But there's a healing effect that takes place when we're on or near a river, lake or ocean; it cleanses what life on the land does to us, almost as if the water is telling us that it's okay we left it behind, it'll be there waiting for us whenever we need to return. I guess everyone can use a little de-evolvement now and again.

As for me, I'd only experienced lakes before, and those not nearly often enough. I'd spent my life up to this point in Minnesota, where all you had to do was pick a direction and go and you could be lake wet in no time. The state could easily be an island if the water ever got organized and united instead of lounging around scattered all over the place. But despite the thousands of footprints to choose from that Paul Bunyan and Babe the Blue Ox had left behind, I'd only made it to a lake on a handful of occasions, content to spend my days in the city with the rest of the landlocked ants.

But I had greatly enjoyed those few times. I always felt different the moment we pulled away from the dock, more at peace. Unfortunately I'd lost my need for such things somewhere along the way. One of the reasons we humans made it to the top of the food chain, besides being able to manufacture weapons of mass destruction, is our adaptability. You can put one of us in any situation, no matter how extreme, and we'll usually find a way to cope; and for the most part, that's a good thing. But sometimes we adapt in a way that isn't all that healthy, like staying in a harmful relationship. Or job. Or boring ass life. If we don't break out by a certain point, there's a chance we'll never do so, and we simply accept it. We've adapted to our circumstances, when we should be gnawing our leg off to escape like any decent wild animal would. But we humans are civilized, and tend to accept whatever crap is thrown our way, no matter how buried in it we become.

But something wild had come my way, and thus the miracle of my attempt at escape. One of my Facebook buddies had been giving me a hard time when I posted that my next stop would be Cancun, saying it was a tourist trap and that Buffett wouldn't be caught dead there. Which was funny, since I would stumble across a Margaritaville restaurant on my second day, so I'm guessing Jimmy'd been caught there alive at least once or twice. But my friend had missed the entire point of my journeys anyway. I wasn't trying to be Marco Polo, unless it was in a swimming pool full of comely lasses. I didn't need to try to go to unmapped regions; they were all unmapped to me. If I was anyone, I was Ponce De León, looking for my own personal fountain of youth. The way I saw it it could be anywhere, so I might as well look at Señor

Frogs with the rest of the tourists before stomping off into the jungle alone with a machete. I could travel to more exotic locations once I had a little experience under my belt.

Eventually the bus arrived at my hotel, and I disembarked and got settled into my room. I quickly changed into my swim trunks, grabbed my beach towel, and hurried downstairs. I made my way through the lobby, patio, and pool area, taking note of the location of the tiki bar as I passed, and finally came to the end of the concrete. I looked down and paused at this momentous occasion, then kicked off my flip flops and took my first steps onto a tropical beach.

I felt like Neil Armstrong as I left my footprints in that virgin white sand, except the sand of course was hardly a virgin, having endured thousands of feet over the years. But never mine. I had never been on a beach before, by lake or by sea. It felt delicious having my feet surrounded by all those little pieces of rock. I could have stood there for hours, just wiggling my lower digits in the stuff, but I soon discovered just how hot a tropical sun can be, especially to a tenderfoot like me who usually wore shoes three hundred and sixty-two days a year. Those tiny, benign pebbles soon began to feel like tiny, not so benign pieces of molten lava, and I began to do the high quick step towards the nearest lounger, hissing and ouching with every stride.

I dove onto the chair and quickly pulled my feet on board, as if to escape from a hungry school of piranhas, then arranged my towel and kicked back to observe my surroundings.

There was an awful lot to observe, and I was torn between Mother Ocean and a dozen or so nicely filled bikinis peppered around my vicinity. I pulled the mirrored sunglasses I had purchased with just this sort of thing in mind out of my shirt pocket and put them on, then took off the shirt, hoping the glare from my white bod wouldn't blind any nearby sunbathers, or signal any planes passing overhead. The last thing I needed was a Sun Country 727 using me as a landing beacon.

As I alternated my view between the rolling surf and perky bottoms, I slowly became aware of the fact that I was now, quite suddenly, in Mexico. And no matter what anyone says, it is not a small world after all. Imagine yourself standing on the planet, in scale; you wouldn't even amount to a grain of sand on a beach ball. I had now traveled from fairly near the top of that ball almost all the way down to the middle. I looked over my shoulder back at the hotel. Yes, those were palm trees swaying in the breeze where there used to be pine trees buffeting in a blizzard. I breathed in heavily the warm, salty air, and sighed contentedly;

it was almost perfect. There was only one thing missing...

"Buenos dias, señor. Can I bring you something?"

I looked up, and found a waiter in a tropical shirt standing next to my lounger.

"How did you do that?" I said.

"Do what, señor?" he asked.

"Show up on cue like that," I said. "I was just thinking how good a margarita would taste right now, and how I should have gotten one from the bar before coming down here, and what a long hop back it would be to get one. Then it occurred to me it wouldn't do any good to make the trip anyway since I would just spill most of it while racing over the hot coals. I'd almost resigned myself to being thirsty when you showed up to save the day."

Hector smiled (I assumed his name was Hector since that was what his name badge said, but I could have been wrong). "We'll have to take care of that right away," he said. "A margarita for you, then?"

"Yes, please," I said. I watched attentively as he walked over to a couple on my right and took their order, then headed towards the bar and disappeared. He was out of sight for what seemed like an interminable length of time while I sat there salivating, then reappeared with a tray full of drinks, including a nice, big, sweaty, cold, margarita for me which I signed for. I have no idea where he went after that, since all my attention was now focused on my frosty and much anticipated new friend.

I moved the umbrella a bit out of the way and took a sip, and immediately knew it was the best thing I had ever tasted. Like the gumbo in New Orleans. And the Corona on the bus to the hotel. And everything else I would have on my trip. The truth of it was, I was just beginning to understand what taste was all about. New Orleans had been lesson one; this was lesson two. Taste evidently wasn't just about those buds covering your tongue. I could be sitting back in my condo sipping this exact same margarita and it would be, well, good. And that's it. Conversely, I could be sitting here on this beach eating Kraft macaroni and cheese, and it would border on gourmet fare. I suppose the tongue may taste the food, but the brain interprets those tastes. And like an Olympic eastern block skating judge during the cold war, the brain can be biased at times. Especially, as it turns out, when it's happy.

I had four margaritas on the beach that first afternoon; two for my front side, and two for my back. That was my timer for being out in the sun. As quickly as I was downing them I figured it worked out to about thirty minutes per slab of white flesh, and I didn't want to risk much more exposure than that my first time out under Super Sol. After that I donned my shirt, and more importantly, my flip-flops. They may not have stopped my toes from being trampled in New Orleans, but they did wonders for the soles of my feet during my walk up to the poolside tiki bar.

I grabbed a stool, sat down, and ordered another margarita; I really didn't see the point in veering off my tequila and lime soaked course when the seas were so inviting. I took a quick drink from it to get it down past the slop over the side whenever you pick it up level, and that's when I met Quinn.

"Hello," he said, in a somewhat somber tone, at least for a poolside bar in Mexico.

I turned to look at him. He was sitting two stools down from me, an empty one between us. I judged him to be in his early forties, a little gray sneaking into his hair. He wore a silk shirt covered in boat drinks, and I don't mean he'd spilled all over himself; it was just a loud, festive shirt that put my rather tame one to shame. He didn't look particularly happy, in contrast to his attire, and I immediately got the impression he wanted someone to talk to.

Unfortunately, I thought at the time, it appeared he'd picked me, and I really didn't want my tropical parade rained upon.

"Hello," I said back, not wanting to raise the bar of the conversation in the hope he'd get bored and start a new one with the bartender instead, who got paid for putting up with that sort of thing.

"Is that a margarita?" he asked, in an accent from one of those England, Scotland, Australia, or South Africa type places.

"Yes, it is," I said, fondling the base of my glass, which gave me a grip on it in case he meant to steal it.

He motioned to the bartender. "Dos margaritas, por favor," he said, pointing at himself and me.

"Thanks," I said, grateful despite my slight questioning of his motives; if there is one constant in the universe it's that all guys are happy to get a free drink, even if they're not sure why the person is buying it for them.

He stood up and moved one bar stool down to sit next to me; evidently I gave the go ahead for this maneuver when I'd accepted his drink. Then he stuck out his hand to me.

"My name's Quinn," he said.

"Jack," I said, shaking his hand.

The bartender brought us our drinks, which gave me two soldiers in my platoon, and Quinn picked his up. "Cheers, then."

I picked up the more veteran margarita of my two and clinked glasses with him, both of us spilling some over the side in spite of my precaution against such things. "Cheers," I said, and we each took a drink.

"Where are you from?" he asked.

"Minnesota," I said, almost feeling I should add America to it since I wasn't in it anymore. "And you?"

"Guildford," said Quinn. "England."

"Really?" I said. "England? What are you doing all the way down here?"

He looked at me as if to point out what an idiotic question that had been, given the tiki bar in Mexico we were sitting at, his tropical shirt, and the ninety-nine to one tourist ratio in the area. "I'm overseeing the construction of a floating cricket pitch," he said sarcastically, then pointed towards the ocean. "Right out there."

I looked at the water. "Nice place for it," I said, determined not to let him make me feel any stupider than I already did.

"The queen and I thought so," he said. "Just have to outbid the bloody Swedes and their ski resort."

"Good luck with that," I said.

"Thanks," said Quinn. "But seriously; what I'm doing here is looking for someone to go on the piss with. Think you'd be up for it?"

I stared at him, not quite sure now what sort of lunatic I was sitting next to. "Uh, excuse me?"

"Ah. Didn't quite get that, did you?" said Quinn. "Sorry. Let me try American; I'm going to get drunk, and I was hoping you'd join me."

That sounded somewhat more appealing at least. "Well, I've actually already started, so I think *you'd* have to be joining *me*."

"Bollocks," Quinn said. "Behind already, am I? Oh, well. Been that sort of day." He picked up his glass and drained it as I watched, then motioned to the bartender for another.

"Why are you so anxious to get drunk?" I said.

"You mean besides the obvious reasons, such as it's a lot of fun?" said Quinn.

"Yeah, besides that," I said.

Quinn gazed out onto the beach as if he was looking for something. "There," he said at last. "You see that girl?"

"I see lots of girls," I said, which I did.

"Not those girls. I'm talking about the one snogging the guy on the lounger," said Quinn.

Snogging I got, having seen my Harry Potters. I shielded my eyes with my hand against the glare of the sun, and looked towards where he was pointing. "Oh. That one," I said. It was hard to see what she looked like, as tangled up as she and her boy toy were. "What about her?"

"That would be my girlfriend," said Quinn. "Or at least, the woman I came down here with."

"Ouch," I said. "Sorry."

"My fault for being such a wanker," Quinn said. "I might have known she'd run off with the first young bloke she met."

"So, you knew this was going to happen?" I said.

"I should have, as young as she is. But since I paid for her ticket and her room, the least she could have done was be more discreet about it," Quinn said.

I put my sunglasses on again in hopes of getting a better look at her, but it didn't help; there were too many body parts intertwined to make any sense of the human pretzel. They looked like two strings of Christmas lights you carefully put in the box last year, only to find them hopelessly tangled the next. "How old *is* she?" I asked, curious.

"Twenty, I think," said Quinn.

"Wow," I said, looking at him and wondering how he had managed to pull off such a feat. "That is a wee bit young, I guess."

"Well, I'm having my midlife crisis so I have an excuse," said Quinn.

"Really?" I said, almost excitedly, happy to find a potential cohort. "It's possible I might be having one of those myself."

"Are you sure?" asked Quinn, skeptically. "Have you started dating women young enough to be your daughter?"

"No, but I broke up with my girlfriend," I said.

"And did you buy a red Porsche?" said Quinn.

"Nope," I said. "A beat up red Cadillac. But it is a convertible."

"Hm," said Quinn. "I don't really know if that gets you into the club; we're pretty exclusive. Any thing else that might strengthen your resume?"

"Besides quitting the job I'd been working for nine years, selling my condo and everything I own, and hitting the road to enjoy myself?" I said.

It was Quinn's turn to look at me. "Yes, besides all that," he said dryly.

I though about it. "No, that's about it," I said.

"Well, as a member of the Midlife Crisis Club let me deliberate with myself for a moment about your pending membership," said Quinn. "Be right back." He turned away from me and began talking to himself. "Yes. Well, you heard him. Bit of a raving nutter, don't you think? You're right about that, of course. Thumbs up then? Good; I'll let him know." He turned back to face me. "After careful consideration, me, myself, and some other tosser in my head, are happy to announce that you are now a member in good standing in the Midlife Crisis Club."

"Thanks for the confirmation," I said. "Are there any perks that go along with that?"

"Yes; you have the right to act like a complete and total git whenever you feel like it," said Quinn.

"I think I've been doing that for a while now, but it's nice to have the official go ahead," I said.

I had to say I liked Quinn immediately, at least immediately after we got past the language barrier. I thought it might be fun to hang out with him, especially since I didn't have anything better to do. And I was pretty sure I had a grasp of this English thing now.

"Any other questions?" said Quinn.

"Nope. I'm good to go." I said, then picked up my glass, and raised it to the sky. "Let's piss!" I said.

"Close enough, mate," said Quinn. "Close enough."

Chapter 19:
"Party at the middle of the world."

"Olé, olé, olé, olé..."

"Olé, olé!"

Our soccer anthem rang out into the night, causing a cargo ship and a pod or two of dolphins to veer off course and steer clear of the coastline.

Quinn and I stumbled along the beach, sharing both a bottle of tequila and the bond that only two obnoxiously inebriated, heterosexual men can share.

I stopped and took a swig from the bottle, no longer able to safely both walk and drink at the same time. I passed it to Quinn, who took a sloppy gulp, then wiped his mouth with the back of his hand.

"You know what mate?" he slurred at me. "You're alright for a Yank."

"And you're alright for a Brit," I slurred back. "More fun than *my* Brit was, that's for sure." I stopped and thought about it. "Well, most of the time anyway."

"Yeah, well, you're more fun than the Brit I brought down here, too," said Quinn. "Although I'm sure Don Juan is enjoying himself. I hope they shag each other to death."

"I wonder if that's possible," I said thoughtfully, at least as thoughtfully as a days worth of ingesting fermented agave leaves allowed.

"Wouldn't be the worst thing to study," said Quinn.

"I think I'm done studying," I said. "All I've ever done is try and figure things out and it never got me anywhere."

"It got you here," said Quinn.

I looked around me at here; there was a sky full of stars and a beautiful moon hanging up above. Party barges made there way across the nearby water, lit up like little floating Christmas villages. The waves of the ocean crashed gently on the white sand; I'm sure it wasn't easy to crash gently, but they were doing it with style and grace, never the less. The music of a mariachi band floated down from the hotel patio, providing a more suitable soundtrack for the scene than even our soccer song.

It was all very romantic, and it occurred to me that one of these days I was going to have to try my hand at hanging out in one of these exotic locals with a woman instead of a drunken foreigner, or at the very least, with a drunken foreign woman, so I could have the other sticky and messy kind of fun, too; but not yet. While I certainly could see the merits of a female of my species for companionship, for the time being I was enjoying the simplicity of just hanging out with the guys. There was no pressure, other than the pressure to somehow remain standing.

I came back to Earth, or its alternate Mexican universe equivalent, and Quinn's statement. "I'm not sure if studying or *not* studying got me here," I said.

"But you told me you were doing all this to try and work out your life," said Quinn.

"Yes, but one of the things I'm trying to work out is how to not try and works things out," I said.

Quinn stood staring at me, wobbling back and forth. "You know, mate, sometimes you don't make a whole lot of sense."

"I know," I said, shrugging. "I'd work on it, but like I just told you..."

Quinn weaved quietly about, then said, very seriously, "Never mind. But since we're on the subject of life I have something very important to ask you."

I watched him for a moment, waiting for him to say something, but he remained silent, looking like a robot going into shutdown mode. "Quinn?" I said finally, then when he still didn't respond, I repeated it, only louder. "Quinn!"

He started, then looked at me again.

"You said you had something important to ask me?" I said.

He appeared to think hard for a second, then said, "Yes. I do. It's about all this life business you're worrying about. Listen," he said, then leaned close to me, almost falling over in the process. "Do you know what the most important thing to remember is? The one thing you have to do to enjoy living? The simple key to eternal happiness? Do you know what that is, Jack?"

"No," I said. "No, I don't."

Quinn looked disappointed. "Neither do I," he said. "Don't have a bloody clue, actually."

"Thanks for getting my hopes up," I said.

"No problem," said Quinn. He handed me the tequila bottle. "Now that we have that worked out, I'm going to go vomit and pass out."

Quinn staggered off towards the hotel, walking at least two steps side to side for every step forward, until he finally disappeared out of sight.

"Bye," I said. I plopped my ass in the sand and my toes in the water, and sat the bottle down next to me. Now that Quinn had suddenly abandoned me, more tequila didn't sound appealing, and it certainly would have been redundant. I felt tired and wanted to lay back, but knew if I did, the next thing I would see would be the sunrise. Either that or the back of a dune buggy bouncing off after rolling over me. Instead I put my arms on my knees and watched the ocean and sand play.

It had been fun whooping it up with Quinn today; dancing in a conga line while a bartender poured tequila in my mouth from a gas can had been just one of the highlights. But it was good to be alone now, too. It was still a new sensation for me; I'd experienced it a bit on the drive down to New Orleans, but it was different here because I felt so very far from home.

It all could have been an away mission to a new world with Captain Kirk, minus a couple of guys in red shirts about to have their hemoglobins sucked out by a carnivorous gas cloud. All the strange, spiky flora I'd seen on the walk to the Cancun Margaritaville. The three foot long, hissing green lizard who demanded that we walk around him on the street instead of his sidewalk. Which we did, of course; I don't know about Quinn, but it turns out I'm not ready to be confronted by testy iguanas after all. And then there was the amazing sunset I'd watched from my balcony during a short clothes changing break, the sky turning an unearthly shade of pink. It was a lovely planet, this Mexico, to be sure.

I caught sight of something moving out of the corner of my eye down the beach, and I cast my view away from Luna to check it out. It looked at first like a small dog trotting towards me. I would have expected it to be a cha-whooa-whooa given my location, as well as too many Taco Bell ads ingrained in my brain, but it appeared to be much chubbier than that.

As it came closer I realized I had no idea what it was, and a little primeval fear of the unknown rose up inside me. I panicked a bit and reached for my phaser, and prepared to set it for stun, but found only my tequila bottle; I grabbed it anyway, unsure if I was planning to hit the creature or offer it a drink.

Luckily the little alien didn't seem interested in eating me or inhabiting my body. It nonchalantly trotted past me about six feet away, then toddled off on down the beach. I watched it go, my hackles gradually settling back to their original position, and I canceled my red alert status.

I realized it had been an armadillo. I don't know why, but after it was gone it thrilled me to no end, and it gradually became my single favorite memory of Mexico. It was funny how things worked out. For starters, that seeing the little bugger left a bigger impression than all the tropical beauty around me; it may have had to do with my state of mind, or lack there of, at the time. And if I'd never met Quinn, I probably wouldn't have even been down on the beach, at least not at that hour. *And* if Quinn hadn't left to go toss out his anchor when he did, my little armored friend probably never would have come near us with all the racket we were making. So if Quinn and I hadn't drank enough tequila to make Alcoholics Anonymous put us on their most wanted list, I never would have had that tiny little memory I now cherished so much.

It just goes to show that every moment has the potential to be a memorable one, and often when we least expect it.

Three *"Olés"* for tequila, and for my new friend Quinn.

And viva la Mehico.

Chapter 20:
"Mistakin' Jamaicans."

"George Clooney! It's George Clooney, mon!"

I'd been hearing it all day, everywhere I went. On the beach, in the shops, on/in the beach shops.

"Hey, hey, look everyone! We got George Clooney over here!"

It was my third of four days I was spending in Jamaica. Yesterday I'd lounged around all afternoon, just kickin' back next to the ocean, walking up to a little tiki bar for Red Stripes and rum drinks. It had been the most relaxing day of my vacation slash new life so far, and my plans for today weren't that much different; I wasn't going to wander far from my two watery friends.

The ocean in Jamaica is amazingly blue, meaning it tends to be green. It was the same thing in Mexico, a magnificent, calmly rolling sea of sparkling turquoise. When I scooped some up in my hand I half expected it to be colored, but of course it wasn't (in truth it was, but I couldn't hold enough to see it).

I didn't know at first which of those two of my Caribbean destinations had had more beautiful beaches, waters, and sunrises and sets. But I figured it out later; it was whichever one I was standing on at the time. They may have both been a little touristy and visiting them wasn't exactly exploring uncharted waters, but it didn't matter; the beach was the beach, the ocean was the ocean, and the place where the two meet is magical.

And though I don't know for sure if I would call it magical, I do know now why Jimmy would risk life and limb for Jerk Chicken. I really think we should have stopped at cavemen ways and just grilled everything. And again, spice, spice, spice. If I had been a pirate tooling around the Caribbean back in the day, that's what I would have been after; the hell with gold doubloons, give me yer allspice, cayenne, cumin, and cilantro. And while ye be at it, hand over your peppers and onions, matey!

"Look, pretty ladies, it's George Clooney! Come and say hello!"

Okay, this was beginning to get weird.

Like I mentioned before, I like to think I look like George Clooney. I like to *think* that. I don't for a moment believe it's true, however. Oh, maybe if someone had lost their glasses and was drunk, standing a half a mile away while looking into the sun, they might for a very fleeting moment think I could be him. But to be honest, I'm just an average Joe in reasonable shape who isn't going to repulse anyone, as opposed to one of God's gifts to women.

So it was a little odd that almost everywhere I went today, eating a hearty Jamaican breakfast, wandering through the marketplace looking for treasures, stopping to get yet another Jerk drumstick at a roadside stand, there were Jamaicans pointing me out as George Clooney. I'm not saying I minded, mind you. I'm just saying it was weird.

I finished my chores for the day and headed towards the beach, happy to lose even my beloved flip-flops when I hit the sand. There's something about all those tiny grains of seashells and rocks between your toes that give you happy feet, as long as they haven't turned into hot coals as they did a couple of times over in Mehico. Of course those same little grains can get annoying as hell when they end up in your bed, but while you're on the beach they can hang out anywhere they like, as long as they don't get too personal.

I arrived back at the same spot I'd spent most of yesterday in, and found my favorite wooden beach lounger available and waiting most invitingly. I knew I was supposed to be traveling around seeing new places but I figured there was nothing wrong with seeing the same new place today as long as it was still new, and I didn't want to mess with a good thing; the sun and surf might not be so perfect a few yards down the beach. Besides, my tiki bar was right there within walking distance even for someone who was fast becoming as lazy as I was. I headed straight for the latter and found my mon, Jimarcus, back on duty.

"Good afternoon! How did you sleep?" he said.

"Face down, in a puddle of drool," I said.

Jimarcus laughed. "Ya, drinkin' as much rum as you did can do that to a person."

"Was I that messed up?" I asked.

"Let me just say you were the life of the party here. You made quite a few friends, I tink," said Jimarcus.

"Hm," I said. "Is that good or bad?"

"Good, mon! You were so friendly you were almost Jamaican. But I don't know how your pocketbook felt about it; it took quite a beatin'" said Jimarcus.

"Ugh," I said. Oh, well. Not so easy come, much easier go.

"Can I get you something to drink?" asked Jimarcus. "A Red Stripe or a rum and coke?"

I considered his kind offer. My body had been acting like it was hooked up to a metronome all morning, bad, good, bad, good, and it was swinging back to bad right now. "I'm not feeling all that much better than my wallet at the moment," I said. "How about a Bloody Mary, instead?"

"Comin' right up," said Jimarcus. He did his thing and slid me my drink, and I got out my wallet to pay. "No, mon; this one is on me."

"Thanks," I said. Now I was really worried. I like to take care of my bartenders and waitresses, but when they start giving you free drinks after a wild night you have to wonder what the hell you did to deserve it.

I stumbled my way over to my lounger and collapsed, suddenly quite dizzy and glad to be back in the prone position. This was becoming one of these sneaky bastard hangovers. You wake up and you don't feel all that great, but once you start moving around it almost goes away and you're optimistic about your recovery chances. But the hangover isn't gone; it's hiding in the bushes, stalking you, waiting for the moment you least expect it to pounce and rip your stomach to shreds and bang your head against the nearest rock. I wasn't quite that bad yet, but I could tell my battle was far from over.

I took a sip from the Bloody. It helped a little bit immediately, though my taste buds weren't all that thrilled with the alcohol they sniffed out, and I wished Scotty was around to just beam the whole thing past them and into my stomach where it would do the most good. I leaned back and closed my eyes, hoping to be able to do sixty-second catnaps between sips.

"Look at dat, sexy George Clooney, right here on my beach!"

I opened one eye, and a pretty, young, Jamaican woman who looked vaguely familiar flashed me a warm smile and waved as she walked past. I took a big, long drink of my Bloody Mary. Maybe if I could push through and get drunk again things might start making sense.

"George! There you are, mon. Been lookin' all over for ya. Should have known you'd be right here."

I opened my other eye and found Benjamin coming towards me across the sand. Benjamin was a warm, friendly Jamaican I had met yesterday and become acquainted with. "It's my spot," I said, which it was. I'd even taken a picture of my feet as they rested at the end of the white chair so I could remember the view of my day.

"I see that," said Benjamin. "Well, I got everything arranged for ya. I'm borrowing my brother's car, so we can go any time you're ready."

To where, was the next question in a day rapidly filling up with them. "Uh, you're going to have to refresh my memory, Ben."

Benjamin looked me over, then laughed. "You don't remember, do you mon?" he asked, obviously delighted by the fact.

"Actually, no. No clue," I said.

146

"You told me you wanted to go to the Appleton Plantation and see where they make all the rum you were drinking. You know, the rum you couldn't figure out why it was tasting so good?" said Benjamin.

"Ah, that rum," I said.

"Benjamin! Get George's autograph for me, okay?" asked an older Jamaican with a head full of dreadlocks, as he walked past.

"Alright, what the hell is going on?" I said.

"What do you mean?" asked Benjamin.

"Why does everyone keep calling me George Clooney?" I said. "I know you have movies, and I know you can see, so I know you can see that he don't look like me," I added, in my best Dr. Seuss rhyme.

"You don't remember that either, mon?" asked Ben.

"No, I don't," I said. "Wait a minute, what don't I remember this time?"

"We were sitting up at the tiki bar last night, everyone talking and having a good time, and you were hitting on a couple of young ladies from Stanford University. It wasn't going very well; it may have had to do with the rum you kept spilling all over yourself."

"Oh, hell," I thought.

"You got all depressed after they left, and I and my friends were trying to cheer you up. But you said what you really needed was for everyone to see you

147

like you did when you looked in the mirror, and that was like George Clooney. So we all started calling you George to make you happy, which worked, and you just kept buyin' drinks," explained Benjamin. "I tink you'll be George now until you go home."

"*Well, that explains a lot,*" I thought to myself. Both my present state of Georgeness and my wallet's apparent slim down. But what the heck; it was what I'd always wanted, even if everyone was just saying it to make me feel good. It's not wise to look a gift horse in the mouth too closely; you may get bit.

"Alright. George I am. And I bet *he's* not on a beach in Jamaica right now," I said, getting up from my chair. "Let's go sample some rum."

"No, he's probably in Monaco eating caviar and wooing some princess," said Benjamin.

"You're probably right," I said, as we walked towards the road. Maybe George and I could do a prince and pauper thing someday. But then I looked around me; trade my beach for a palace? Not a chance. My jerk chicken for fish eggs? No way. Benjamin for a princess? Hm...

Well, two out of three ain't bad, I guess.

Chapter 21:
"The weather isn't here, but it's still beautiful."

Water was falling from the sky.

It had been doing so all day and into the night, this departure from the 24/7 paradise I had become accustomed to over the last week or so. The thought had never occurred to me that it might actually rain in the tropics, which is supremely naive of course, but I was already good and spoiled.

I was sitting on my hotel balcony which overlooked the beach, and coincidentally, the ocean. The rain was falling at a perfect angle so I wasn't getting wet, and it was actually quite pleasant. I did have a few pangs of regret the next day over not spending my last few hours as an honorary George Clooney with my new Jamaican drinking buddies, but I needed a break from all out fun. And I liked the symmetry of it anyway. Roughly a month ago I'd been sitting out on my balcony in Minneapolis in the snow, coming to the realization that I was seriously not happy in the head. Now I was sitting out on my balcony in Jamaica in the rain, and coming to the realization that I was seriously just the opposite. I was feeling good and enjoying the sensation.

It had been a great stay. I'd squeezed in more variety in Jamaica than I had during my visit to

Mexico, which had consisted mostly of eating Mexican food and drinking Coronas and tequila. My first day in Jamaica I'd tried my hand at surfing, for example. How did I do? Well, Sheriff Woody said that Buzz Lightyear couldn't fly, that he just fell with style; I should be so lucky while surfing. I kept hearing the song *Wipe Out* in my head every time I did some crazy and disastrous new maneuver that would have made the *Wide World of Sports* agony of defeat skier proud. It was still fun though, and I'd like to maybe try it again some time. That is, unless I decide to stick to a sport my coordination is more suited to, such as beach towel lying on.

Benjamin, my Jamaican guide and friend, also took me to Rick's Cafe, which is probably the best known bar in Negril, if not in all of Jamaica. It sits on a western cliff overlooking the ocean, and has a beautiful view of said waters. But what Rick's is most famous for is cliff jumping, which is just as it sounds; jumping off of cliffs. Into the ocean at least, as opposed to Wiley Coyote and his numerous splats while chasing the Roadrunner.

The main cliff is about thirty feet above the water, although they had a professional diving for tips from a wooden plank nailed to a tree about ninety feet up. It made me dizzy just watching him, but he survived, and it was thrilling and amazing to see.

There are also a couple of shorter cliffs, right around ten feet high. I tried each of them and enjoyed the experience, and managed not to break myself in the process, and that was going to be it for me; I had no intention of going near the thirty footer. Benjamin himself said it was a bad idea since I'd never dived before, and that people got hurt all the time jumping, some of them quite badly. So my well developed sense of self preservation kicked in and just said no.

But then a group of younger people from Philadelphia I'd been talking to got it into their heads to start egging me on to try the big jump, obviously wanting to see the sort of maiming they could talk about for years to come. It's astonishing what a little peer pressure can do to lower your IQ, even from people who aren't really your peers. In no time at all I found myself waiting behind two guys and a gal from their group to hurl myself into oblivion. It took the first lad a couple of moments to get up the nerve, but eventually he dove off screaming, and gravity did the rest. The second guy didn't hesitate; the minute the first guy was out of his way he jumped with a happy shout, totally embracing the young and invincible thing.

The girl, however, got to the edge and froze, despite the yelling of her friends and the rest of the crowd below; perhaps if someone would have had some beads to throw to her she would have had more reason to go. I decided if she chickened out I would gallantly escort her back down to her pals and fowl out myself; the whole thing seemed like an extraordinarily bad idea now that I was up there. I'd worked on the fourth floor of Image Makers for years, and there'd been many a time I would have been happy to throw myself out the nearest window and onto the concrete parking lot below. But here on the cliffs I found I lacked any incentive to risk bodily harm. So I was quite relieved to find a soul mate in my cowardice.

But then the girl did the unthinkable. She backed away from the cliff and turned, as if to walk away, then suddenly whirled, ran, and leaped off the brink with a high pitched shriek that lasted until she hit the water. I'd been deserted. I felt like the last lemming, who now had no one to back him up in his desire to buck his stereotype. There was nothing left to do.

So I baby stepped up to the edge and peeked over. It's peculiar how much more dangerous thirty feet straight down looks than thirty feet straight ahead. And how much more difficult it appears to travel, when I suspect that in reality the only energy it would take would be the calories I'd burn while flailing my arms around and screaming like a little girl. But the real problem is liftoff. Once you get into open space there isn't much effort involved, other than trying to land in such a way as to avoid weeks of traction. But the choice is made at that point and there's no turning back. Like everything else in my life it came down to a decision, and like everything else in my life I didn't want to make it.

I stood staring down at the beautiful aqua colored agua, thinking this could be one of those life changing moments I'd heard about, where one little step out of a plane or off a bridge had changed everything. And when I finally realized what I had to gain by leaping, I stepped back away from the edge, saluted the crowd, and proudly walked down the stairs to the much expected heckles of my Philadelphia non-peer group.

Why didn't I jump? Well, besides being a yellow bellied former desk jockey, I didn't much see the point. Yes, if I would have leapt and survived I might have found a new vigor for life. But I thought I already had one, and how many did I need? I wasn't collecting them, and risking my neck to win a spare didn't seem worth it to me.

But the trip to Rick's wasn't a total loss. After my fall from grace Benjamin and I sat down and drank with my eggers-on while I wore the bev-nap of shame they fashioned for me. And I got to see yet another gorgeous Caribbean sunset, this one from a perfect viewpoint. And I did somewhat redeem my courage the next day when I went parasailing, even if I kept a weather eye open the whole time for schools of sharks, barracudas, or jellies I might fall into. Sorry, I just can't help myself.

Tomorrow I'm renting a car and driving all the way to Kingston, from where I'll be taking my late afternoon flight back to New Orleans. I wanted to leave from there instead of Negril so I could make one last stop before leaving the island, but as it turns out I'll be making two.

My first and always planned visit is to the Bob Marley home and museum. I've always respected Mr. Marley and what he and his music stood for, and I wanted to feel a bit more connected to him. *"Light up the darkness."* We could use a few more people trying to do just that.

And my last stop? The Red Stripe Brewery for a tour. Why? Because as they say in the commercials, Red Stripe and reggae have been helping their white friends dance for over seventy years, and I'd been one of the recipients of their aid over the last few days.

And because it's beer.

Hooray beer!

Chapter 22:
"I heard he was in town."

Jimmy Buffett. You hear the name and immediately it brings to mind beaches and bars, like some Pavlovian response. Singer, songwriter, author, entrepreneur; Jimmy rules over his laid back, tropical realm like a benevolent king on a bamboo throne.

And never was a king more deserving of his crown. One of the reasons Jimmy's subjects are so loyal is because he never stopped giving them what they wanted, followed by more and more of the same. How many performers are willing to play the same eight to ten songs concert after concert, year after year, and even manage to genuinely enjoy doing so? And don't forget Jimmy's books, which are like longer versions of his songs, just as lyrical and just as musical. Between all the albums and novels a citizen of Buffett Island can lose themselves in his words and world for hour upon hour.

And if after all the listening and reading you decide you'd like to physically immerse yourself in one of Jimmy's stories, you can always stop by one of the Margaritaville bar/restaurants located in your choice of vacation destinations. It used to bother me there wasn't a Margaritaville near me, say perhaps in the Mega Mall, so we frozen Minnesotans would have a place to thaw out now and again. And maybe there will be one day. But it occurred to me that there's a certain logic to their location as it stands now. If there had been a Margaritaville in the mall for example, all I'd have had to do to visit it would be to get in the car and drive there, then make my way past a hundred or so shoe stores. It just wouldn't seem that special. And for anyone that happens to live near one already I'm sure that's how it is for them too, but it also means they live somewhere a lot more interesting than most of us to begin with. Montego Bay, Cancun, Key West, Waikiki, Myrtle Beach, and the New Orleans location I'd spent an evening in; it's as if Jimmy is telling us that if we want to come to one of his restaurants, he's gonna make us go on vacation to do so. Now *that's* a caring monarch.

I guess I haven't actually said all that much about Jimmy and whether or not I'm a big fan, or if I proudly wore the title of Parrot Head. I definitely hinted at it here and there, and the fact that I'm making an effort to live my life like his songs should be a dead giveaway. I wouldn't put my hat on sideways, then go stomping off angrily to try and live my life like an Eminem song for example, no matter how fed up I was. Although it might be a valid response to life nowadays for some people, it's just not me. But Jimmy's music has always struck a chord, even if it had only sunk into me as deep as the listening level before, meaning I never considered using it as a handbook for a new lifestyle. That is, until now.

So being an admitted Parrot Head who was out on the road trying to hunt down Jimmy's elusive blue macaw of happiness, I pretty much had to take a little side trip after leaving New Orleans, and stop into Pascagoula, Jimmy's hometown. It wasn't really out of my way anyway, and it got me off the main highway, which was always good; you don't get to see much from those things.

When I arrived I realized I now once again had it officially backwards. Jimmy took off from here for parts unknown and for me these *were* the parts unknown I had taken off to go to; I guess in a way we'd traded places. I took an hour to just drive around and imagine that maybe he'd wheeled his old red bike to that service station for air or ducked into the brick corner store for a box of Junior Mints. Or that maybe he'd been born in the hospital I came across. I could almost envision that Christmas night; the town all decked out for the holidays, the snow not even considering the idea of falling, and the hospital staff not having a clue what the hell they had just helped start. The least they could have done was broken out a blender and whipped up some Christmas margaritas.

Maybe they did, and maybe Jimmy got an early and unofficial baptism.

After reminiscing about Jimmy's hometown for a while, I moved on down the coast to Pensacola and his hotel. Jimmy's hotel; it must seem odd to him, a boy from Mississippi, to stand and look at the thing and know that it was his. I'd be lucky to fill a one room flea infested flophouse named after me and my lifestyle. But there it was, the Margaritaville Beach Hotel. To be honest, I was a little skeptical as I pulled in. It seemed, well, *too* nice, and there is such a thing as far as I'm concerned. But I was wrong this time.

Yes, the place is gorgeous. And elegant, which is something I never thought I could be attracted to, unless it was a she. But this was a very simple, Caribbean clean elegant. The hotel almost blends into the beaches and waters it sits between, everything white and blue and filled with light and air. Even when you're inside you feel like you're outside, sort of a new and relaxed version of inside out. And for another version of inside out try kicking back in the Land Shark Landing on the beach for an hour or six; I did. After all, you can only sit in the sun for so long, but you can sit in an open air bar as long as you want, at least until they tell you to it's time to leave.

It was a relaxing day and a half, spent just moseying around the hotel and beach (and bar). I thought about wandering to the pier down the shoreline to see if there was a fat man on the dock selling popcorn, but I was too lazy; maybe next time.

Seeing Pascagoula, Pensacola, and the rest of Jimmy's stomping grounds along the coast told me a little, I think, about why he is who he is, or at least why it made it easier for him to turn out the way he did. It would have been damned difficult to be Jimmy from Minneapolis; hell, I had his songs for CliffsNotes and I still wasn't sure I was approaching the whole *lay back and enjoy* thing right. But the Gulf emanates something special, and if you grow up there I think it bombards you with a kind of crazy honky-tonk tiki cowboy surfer-dude vibe that messes with your head, in a good way.

Obviously, Jimmy spent a lot of time down there, and I thank the stars for that.

And I know that Jimmy does too.

Chapter 23:
"Ragtop night."

I was in my Caddy driving on the highway in northern Florida, somewhere between Jacksonville and Tallahassee. I had the top down, the air rushing over me as I headed east by southeast. It was late in the afternoon, the sun sitting low in the sky, making its last minute preparations before disappearing beneath the horizon to sleep. The effects of the whirlwind of sights, smells, sounds, and snacks I'd been experiencing for the last week was finally dying down, and I was left alone in my car to think.

There's a solitude to being on the road that's like no other; I think it's a combination of many things, not the least of which is a feeling of complete freedom. Your little rolling world is all your own, not unlike being in a boat out on the water. When you get in your vehicle and drive off you know you are going to be by yourself until you stop and get out again, unless you swing by a Taco Bell drive-thru window. It's a rare thing these days to find a spot outside of our own home that isn't crawling with other people; most of the time we need to make an effort just to be alone. But our cars, trucks, motorcycles, and motor homes are always waiting to grant us sanctuary from the rest of the human race.

Maybe that's part of the reason we have a relationship with our vehicles like we have with no other machine in our lives. The television doesn't even come close; it's a babysitter that we sit in front of and observe, not unlike sitting in front of a window while watching the world go by. With our cars there's a symbiotic connection, and when we sit in that driver's seat it's almost like being in the saddle of a horse. The open range awaits us, whether it be the far side of the continent or the parking lot of the Piggly Wiggly just down the street.

As the planet rolled on beneath my tires I looked back on my trip so far. There was absolutely no doubt in my mind I was enjoying myself. For starters, I'd met some new people, which was a nice change of pace. Other than clients, I had rarely socialized outside of my small circle of friends and coworkers up in Minnesota. I suppose that's natural; most everyone has their little clique they tend to run with. But I was happy not to be gabbing with the same people about the same things for a while. I did have to admit I missed talking to Marty, though, other than the occasional post on Facebook. I guess you can't have everything.

New Orleans had been a kick, and pretty much right to the head. There had been plenty of things to do during the day, and even without the nightlife it would have been well worth the visit. But when a city is as good at throwing a party as the Big Easy was, you should try not to miss it, and I was glad I got to be on their guest list for a few nights.

Spending a total of eight days in Jamaica and Mexico hadn't exactly hurt my mental health either, or the amount of melanin I was currently showing off. My skin was already a few shades darker than it had been at any time since, well ever. Maybe I'd soaked up enough sun for a good farmer tan while gallivanting around the neighborhood as a kid, but never an almost all over beach type tan. When I inspected myself in the rear view mirror it was nice to see a healthy looking me staring back, as opposed to the pale rider with the fluorescent infused packaging I was used to.

So I guess the operative phrase in my Buffett themed musical was so far, so good. But my money was only going to last for so long and when it ran out I was going to have to settle in to some sort of a lifestyle somewhere. Unfortunately I wasn't creative enough to run around and have a good time, record a song about it, and repeat the process indefinitely like certain singers I knew. Unless I suddenly met my muse while sitting under a banana tree drinking rum, I was going to have a severe cash flow problem, sooner or later.

That meant I was going to have to deal with the whole *me and my life* dilemma again. It was one thing to be on an extended holiday, which was more or less what I was doing right now. Traveling and having a great time would distract me from my problems as long as I could keep it up, but what then? It was the same burden people often put on their vacations, the hope that a week of fun will heal whatever ails them. I suppose sometimes it does, and it sure as hell can't hurt. But usually we just go back to square one, and my square was someplace I didn't ever want to be trapped inside again.

I looked over towards the western horizon where the sun was saying its final goodbyes for the day, radiant splashes of red and gold painting the sky. Clouds are like actors on a stage; an author can pen the most beautiful screenplay, but if no one plays the parts it never comes to life. In the same way the sun can shine all it wants to in an empty sky, but to put on a truly gorgeous sunrise or sunset it needs the clouds to show off its myriad of colors. Luckily for me, everyone had shown up at the theater tonight, and the evening's performance was a grand one.

It was almost impossible to look at a sky like the one I was seeing and be negative, even for a crackerjack pessimist like I used to be. Normally I'd be all over the chance to agonize about some good, pending doom I'd cooked up, but today I felt different.

I wasn't able to put the thought of my lurking

future entirely out of my mind at first, however. But I did manage to leave it standing out in the front yard while I peeked at it through a crack in the curtains. I could tell it was puzzled by not being ushered right inside in the usual manner, like a welcome house guest. It tentatively walked up and tried the front door, the entrance all my negative thoughts were accustomed to using, but this time it found it tightly locked. It knocked and rang the bell several times but I ignored it, and eventually it wandered away for a few moments, only to come back as a worry about money and try to climb in a window. This too was locked, and after one more lame attempt to gain access through the chimney disguised as my mother, it slunk away to try and figure out whose brain this was, and what had been done with my regular one.

The fact was I simply couldn't care about anything at the moment. Sure, there was a good chance I'd take the time eventually to anguish over my tomorrows, but I decided to do it tomorrow. It didn't matter right now, not when and where I was, driving alone in an open top Caddy under a dazzling canopy of fire, a show slowly exiting its stage to make way for night's own starry review. It was a breakthrough for me, to have the time and solitude to worry about something and to choose not to do so. Perhaps I was making progress in my attempt to evolve into a more advanced form of human being after all.

I stuck my head out the side of the car like a dog, letting the wind whip past me as I drove; I would have let my tongue loll if I'd known how. Instead, I opened my mouth, and took a deep breath of fresh, Florida air.

And promptly sucked in a bug.

I don't know what kind, since I immediately swallowed it out of instinct. But even ingesting unidentified flying insects couldn't dampen my spirits, and it actually made me laugh when I thought about it. Yes, it may have shocked me a bit, but I could imagine the surprise the bug had felt at the whole ordeal, and I was fairly glad our roles hadn't been reversed.

The truth was, I felt just plain stupidly happy, and nothing was going to change that. Not tonight at least.

Red sky at night, sailor's delight.

I guess they were right.

Chapter 24:
"The Captain and the bird."

I had a strange dream last night; in a way, I suppose that's not saying much. How many times do we have a normal dream? I don't recall ever waking up and remembering having spent my eight sleeping hours working on an ad campaign, for example. If I did dream about working on an ad campaign, I'd dream about doing it naked. Or while being chased through the water by a flotilla of terribly vicious hamsters. Or both. And if you don't think *that's* terrifying, think again.

This particular dream I had though, didn't involve hamsters. And no one was naked, which unfortunately is usually the case in my dreams, unless it's me. But it did involve water. I was on a sailboat, sailing through stormy seas. I didn't know at first if I was on an ocean or a lake; all I knew was I was getting tossed around pretty good, and some of the waves were cresting higher than my head.

The strange thing was, well, one of the strange things anyway, that the seas were very warm. Not just warm, more like hot, really. Steam literally rose from the waves. They were also quite bubbly, which was even more odd. That ruled out the waters of both Jamaica and Mexico, since although both had been

166

quite balmy, neither of them were carbonated. It took me a bit to work it all out, but after studying the distant, strange, smooth, aqua blue cliffs that surrounded me, I realized that I was floating in a hot tub.

There was, of course, no clue as to why I was in a sailboat in the middle of a storm tossed hot tub; there never is in dreams. But regardless of what got me out there, things weren't going so well, and it was obvious I'd done my sailing classes online. My craft was taking on water, and I had no idea which rope to pull on to make the boat go wherever it was I was trying to go. I noticed I wasn't wearing a life jacket, and since things weren't looking very promising, I leaned down to search under the seats for a life preserver donut thingie. And that's when my boat struck land, and my head struck the wooden seat.

I looked up while rubbing my noggin, and found myself beached on a lovely little tropical island, the sun suddenly having popped out to warm the day. A soft breeze rustled the palms that peppered the sand, as colorful birds flew between them.

I stepped out of the boat to further survey my surroundings; there weren't many signs of life around, other than a path into the palm forest with a red and white striped bar blocking its entrance. I walked over to it and found a little wicker basket hanging from it with a sign that read *"Toll road: $2.50"*, which I'm sure was a reference to the bazillion toll booths I'd encountered while braving the Florida Turnpike.

I checked the pockets of my boat shorts and was relieved to find exactly ten quarters there. I dropped them into the basket and the bar raised, and I started walking down the path. Eventually it led to a small clearing, in which sat a little bamboo hut that would have done the crew of the Minnow justice. I went over and poked my head inside to look around, but as I did so, I heard a voice squawk out to me from behind. At least I assumed it was squawking out to me; all it said was, "Hey, you!", but it was enough to make me turn around in the doorway and look back outside.

That was when I noticed the hammock tied between a couple of palm trees. I hadn't noticed it before because it hadn't been there; my mind was busily filling the set as the play went along. There was a large, bright red parrot wearing a straw hat and sunglasses kicking back in the hammock, and I walked towards him, wishing I had a really big saltine. As I grew closer he hopped out onto his feet and stood before me; he was intimidating, this six foot bird, and he didn't seem very pleased to see me.

"You!" he snapped at me squawkily. "What are you doing on my island?"

I involuntarily took a step backwards. "I-I don't know," I stammered. "You see, I was in sailing in this hot tub, and-"

"Of course you were sailing in a hot tub!" the parrot said. "How else would you get to my island? I want to know why you're here and what you want."

I tried to remain calm and think; his beak looked awfully sharp, as if he could open Corona bottles by simply biting the ends off of them. "I don't know what I want," I said, finally. "I've been trying to figure that out for some time now."

The parrot looked at me irritably. "You're another one of *those*, eh?"

"I'm afraid so," I said.

"Crap!" he squawked. "Why do you idiots always end up here?"

"I don't know," I said.

He sighed. "Well, shit. Nothing I can do about it now, I guess. Follow me, and make yourself useful." He spread his wings, which startled me a bit, then flapped across the clearing and landed on a bar stool that had conveniently materialized in front of a tiki bar that had also conveniently materialized. "Get over here and make me a margarita," he demanded.

I walked over and went around behind the bar, which appeared to be fully stocked with everything you might need to make some liquid happiness. I was having trouble remembering what went into a margarita, though I knew tequila was involved, so I began searching for it amongst the bottles.

"What are you doing?" the bird demanded after a moment.

"Trying to find the tequila," I said, continuing my search.

"Oh for heaven's sake," he squawked. "It's right in the front on the rail; the third bottle from the left."

I lifted up the bottle he had described and looked at it. "This is gin," I said.

"*Your* left, dummy!" he said.

I put the gin back and grabbed the other bottle, which was indeed tequila, and poured a bit into the blender that sat in the center of the bar.

"More!" said the bird.

I added a bit more and put the bottle back down.

"More!" he said angrily. "Are you implying I can't handle my liquor?"

"No!" I said. "I just didn't know...look, if you want it a certain way, then why don't you come back here and make it yourself," I suggested.

He spread his wings and flapped them around at me. "You see any fingers here?" he snapped.

"No. No, I don't," I admitted.

"Then get on with it!" he said impatiently.

I sighed, then picked up the tequila again and slopped a hefty pour into the blender. I looked at the bird and waited for him to complain, but he didn't, so I began searching for the triple sec.

"Now what?" he said, when I didn't find it immediately.

"Triple sec," I said, between gritted teeth.

"Forget it; I don't have time to talk you through while you bumble around with that *and* the lime juice," he said. "Just grab the mix."

I wondered briefly what he would taste like rubbed with some jerk seasoning and grilled over an open flame, then found the Margaritaville mix and poured what I thought should be the right amount into the blender. "How's that?" I said.

"A little late to ask me now, isn't it?" he said, folding his wings grumpily in front of him. "It'll have to do. Next time, measure!"

"I could have sworn you were in a hurry," I said under my breath.

"What was that?" he asked sharply.

"Nothing," I said, then glanced around me for ice.

The bird watched for a moment, then said, "In the cooler, where else!" while waving his wings around as feathers flew. "Geesh!"

I opened the lid of the silver Coleman cooler, and scooped out a handful of ice with my hands and dumped it into the blender.

"Like that was real sanitary," said the bird.

I ignored him and examined the blender, then hit crush, but nothing happened. I stood looking at it stupidly, knowing this latest setback would not sit well with my parrot patron.

"Now what?!" screamed the parrot as more feathers dropped off him; he seemed to be molting on the spot.

"The blender's not working," I said.

"Is it plugged in?!" he screeched.

I leaned down and checked it. "Um, no," I said.

"Then plug it in!" he yelled, as another shower of feathers flew through the air like a colorful Minnesota blizzard.

I quickly did so, and the blender roared to life. "Salt?" I asked.

"I'm a parrot! Of course I want salt!" he said, hoarse from screeching at me.

I salted the rim of a margarita glass, and when the blender stopped, poured the contents into it. Then I sat it on the bar in front of the bird, relieved at having successfully finished my task against all possible odds.

The parrot looked at it, then looked at me, and his red face turned an extra shade redder. He puffed up all his feathers angrily, as if he were about to launch himself at me, but then clutched at his chest with his wings, and quite suddenly fell off his stool.

I hurried around the bar to where he was lying in the sand. He was gasping for air, and I realized he was having a heart attack. He motioned for me to come closer, and I got down on one knee and leaned over him. He lifted his head as far as he could manage and whispered in my ear.

"You-you forgot the umbrella!" he gasped, then went rigid and snuffed it.

And then I woke up.

I'm sure old Sigmund would have a field day with all this, and tell me I have buried feelings about my relationship with my mother. Myself, I might look at it and decide I shouldn't eat jalapeno poppers right before bed. And that I have deep fears of inadequacy when it comes to making margaritas, and better schedule some practice time. And get sailing and hot tubbing to quelch any anxiety in those areas while I'm at it. The best way to deal with your worries is to face them head on, and I was ready for some intense therapy.

Chapter 25:
"Ballad of Crazy Chester."

Let me say this about the difference between alligators and crocodiles; there is none. None that matters, anyway. Not when you're worrying about what's going to happen if you fall off the airboat you're tooling around on in the Florida Everglades. Our guide, Amos, said that a croc has a V-shaped snout, while a gator has a U-shaped one. And that's good information I suppose if you don't want to embarrass yourself around Mr. Dundee. But I have a difficult time imagining myself trying to figure out if it was a U or V shaped row of teeth that was attached firmly to my left leg; I think I would be far too busy screaming bloody murder at the time to care.

I'm not sure what I was thinking when I pulled off of Alligator Alley and signed up for the airboat tour. I hadn't done well in my confrontation with the iguana in Mexico, so why I thought co-mingling with his thirteen foot long carnivorous cousins would be a good way to spend an hour or two is beyond me. But it was something I'd never tried before, so it was supposed to fit in with my new found sense of adventure. One of these days though, I'm going to have to get it through my thick skull that *my* sense of adventure is a bit more of a wuss than most people's.

Alligator Alley, or the Everglades Parkway, is a two lane highway that runs west to east (or east to west, depending on what your heading is) across the southern half of Florida. It's got to be the straightest road I've ever been on, turning only slightly maybe three or four times in about ninety miles. There are alligator and panther crossing signs all along the side of the road, and the latter of the signs startled the daylights out of me. It gave me visions of big black cats crossing my path, or even worse, jumping into the backseat of my open roofed car, and I just *knew* that was going to be bad luck.

But it turns out these panthers are smaller than their jungle cousins, about half the size, and are closer in relation to mountain lions (not that that meant I wanted them chewing on my upholstery). They've also been designated as an endangered species. Personally I think every creature on Earth is endangered having to share the planet with us, but no one would do anything if we slapped the title on all of them. I suppose it's good we keep the club exclusive for that reason, but it would be even better if we didn't have to have the club at all.

Once I'd made it through the Everglades with my interior intact, I turned south and navigated through the outskirts of Miami and headed towards the end of the world. Or at least, the end of North

America, no matter what some people and certain tourist photo spots might try and tell you. The dictionary calls a continent *"the mainland, as distinguished from islands or peninsulas."* Then how can an island or peninsula be part of the continent? When I got to right around Pelican Cay and started seeing water on both sides of me as I drove down Highway A1A, I decided I was no longer in North America and that was that. And though it wasn't the first time this month I'd been out of the country, it was the first time I hadn't needed a passport to get there.

Driving through the Keys with the top down was heaven, and felt like something out of a movie. The sun was beating down on me, the sea breeze filled my lungs, and Jimmy was singing song after song on the stereo, having never sounded better. And of course, my tires were rolling down A1A, which made it even cooler. But the peak thrills came whenever I crossed some long bridge over the ocean. It was a different perspective from being on the beach; I felt almost free of the land, surrounded by water and sky with just a thin piece of road beneath me. The world seemed so vast in those moments and larger than I had ever perceived it before, stretching out in all directions to the horizon. It was oh so very blue, and oh so very beautiful.

I rolled on down my concrete sand bar, passing through Long Key, Conch Key, Duck Key, Grassy Key and a whole lot of other Keys I don't remember. I began to wonder if I might be missing all sorts of interesting little places that weren't on the main road, which was lined mostly with gas stations, motels, and mini malls. I was getting hungry, too, and I couldn't find anything that quite fit whatever it was I didn't know I was looking for.

And then I saw a sign.

It was wooden, weather beaten and small, not much bigger than a mile marker. I have no idea how I even spotted it, surrounded as it was by road signs and manatee mailboxes, which was why I paid attention to it to begin with. I figured I must have been meant to see it, as hidden as it was. And when you find a sign, especially a sign that might be a sign, you better take heed. This particular sign said, *"Crazy Chester's Bar and Boat Stop."*

An ice cold beer to cool me down in the tropical sun sounded doable, and hopefully they served food, too. And even if the name by chance meant only boats could stop in, I figured my Caddy definitely qualified. Besides, I didn't want this Crazy Chester person, if he was indeed crazy, chasing me down the road with a shotgun if I drove on past and ignored his sign. So I slammed on the brakes, sending Maria flying into the windshield once again. The sticky tape holding her in place on the dashboard was losing its gumminess in the heat, a peril for hula girls they don't warn you about. I gently put her back in her spot as I made the turn off of Highway A1A, heading down a narrow, cracked, concrete side road.

It went past a stand of mobile homes on the left and a bunch of auto repair shops on the right, cutting through a jungle of aluminum and steel corrugated buildings. The ocean soon appeared dead ahead of me as I came to the edge of the island, and I followed the curve to starboard since I wasn't sure my Caddy could swim. My destination soon appeared on my port side, and I pulled into the parking lot and shut off the car.

The property was set on the edge and beginning of a small harbor, a flotilla of fishing and sail boats parked in the back yard. The old, small, wooden building looked as if it had been sitting there for a hundred years; I didn't see how it could have become as piled with junk as it was in any shorter stretch of time. Stuffed and mounted fish, surfboards, buoys, nets, sponges, shark jaws, sails, bicycles, oars, airplane propellers, tires, license plates, life preservers and conch shells covered the walls and roof, with the centerpiece being a plaster mermaid languishing on a sofa on the second floor balcony just above the sign. If a hurricane plopped the place down in the middle of your average stretch of Minnesota waterfront real estate, property values would plummet. In other words, it was just the sort of place I'd been looking for.

The building sat up on stilts, and I walked up a flight of wooden stairs and across the front deck before arriving at the screened front door. I could hear Bob Seger singing, *"Roll Me Away"* from inside, but it didn't kick in until the next day how fitting the song had been for me and my arrival. I took note of a sign by the entrance that read simply, *"No shoes, no shirt"*, looking as if the bottom half was broken off and missing, then opened the door and went inside.

The interior was small but nice, at least smaller and nicer than I had expected judging from the outside. There were only a few tables and a small bar with six stools, although I could see through the open windows that there was a little patio balcony in the back with a few more seats. It was decorated a bit like the outside of the building, but not so overwhelming. Mostly I remember ceiling fans creating a pleasant breeze, parrot lights strung across the ceiling, and a brass ship's bell up by the bar, behind which also hung two flags; one a skull and crossbones, the other a Bob Marley freedom flag. Looking at my surroundings, it seemed to me I was in the right place.

I was the only one in the right place, however, so I wandered around the little room a couple of times saying, *"Hello?"* stupidly. I'm not sure why people say hello whenever there's no one there, unless it's supposed to work like a duck call. It didn't do me any good, whatever its purpose, so I walked out the back door to check out the patio.

Outside there was a nice view of the harbor and ocean, and a little bald guy wearing sunglasses and Corona boat shorts sleeping in a lounge chair (the nice view being of the harbor and ocean, not the bald guy). He was holding a half empty Landshark Lager in his hand that rested on his stomach and I felt sorry for it, sitting there getting warm in the heat. It looked awfully tasty, all golden and glistening with sweat in the noonday sun. I was getting ready to clear my throat in hopes of obtaining one for myself, but suddenly the man jumped, as if someone had splashed water on him. I wondered if he could see into the immediate future and it had startled him, since when he jerked he spilled beer all over himself, and perhaps the spill was what made him jump to begin with. All paradoxes aside, he finally noticed me standing there and greeted me, once he got his beer under control.

"Good afternoon!" he said, in a down home and friendly tone.

"Afternoon," I said. "Do you work here?"

"Not when I can help it," he said.

"How about now?" I said. "I was hoping to get one of those Landsharks."

"Then I guess I can't help it," he said, standing up. "Come on inside."

I followed him into the building and he went behind the bar and got me a Landshark from one of the coolers, opened it, and slid it across the bar to where I'd sat down. I took a drink, and it hit the spot I was aiming it at quite nicely.

"Are you the owner?" I said, taking a guess.

"I am," he said. "I'm Chester, and before you ask, yes I am."

That did indeed answer my next question. "I'm Jack. Jack Danielson. And before *you* ask, no, I'm not."

"Well, that got a lot out of the way without saying much," said Chester. "*Now* what are we going to talk about?"

I thought about it. "How long have you owned this place?" I said.

"Oh, about ten years now. That's how long I've been crazy, too, in case you want to know," Chester said.

"So what made you go crazy in the first place?" I asked.

"My friends," said Chester. "One day I was managing a Walmart in Chicago, the next I was withdrawing my life savings and heading south. I was going to go all the way down to Key West, but I stopped in here back when it was still *Crazy Bob's*, and Bob talked me into buying it. For some reason my friends up north all thought I was nuts, and I decided not to argue with them since being sane never got me anywhere. Been crazy ever since."

"Wow, that's great," I said. "You know, I just went crazy myself a couple of weeks ago. You want to hear about it?"

"Sure, why not," said Chester. "But before you begin, are you hungry?"

"Yes, starving," I said. "You do serve food here then?"

"No, I don't," he said.

"Oh," I said, disappointed and confused.

"But can I get you something to eat?" said Chester.

"I thought you just said you don't serve food," I said.

"I did, and I don't," said Chester.

"But you'll get me something to eat, even though you can't," I said, still not getting what the hell he was talking about.

"I didn't say I can't, I just said I don't," said Chester. He leaned over the bar and spoke quietly, in case anyone was listening, although who *anyone* might be in the empty room was beyond me. "I don't have a food service license. In fact, I don't even have a kitchen, other that the one upstairs in my living quarters. But I can cook you up a mean mahi-mahi sandwich on that grill out there," he said, pointing to the patio.

"And how much would-" I began.

"You're not listening," he said.

"Yes I am," I said. "It's just not doing me any good."

"Look, it's no charge, get it? It's free! I can't serve you food 'cuz I don't have a license, but no one says I can't give you some," said Chester.

I felt like telling him there were probably all sorts of people out there in government offices willing to say he couldn't give me food without a license, but I wasn't going to look a gift fish in the mouth. "That's awfully nice of you," I said, instead.

"Can't let you go hungry now, can I?" Chester said. He grabbed some ingredients out of a cooler and cupboard and headed towards the patio. "Be right back."

Chapter 26:
"Little Miss Mahi-Mahi."

An hour later my own story of attempted escape from the ordinary had been told, and my belly was content and full of fresh, delicious seafood. It had been a while since I'd run into someone who wasn't a friend who was willing to give me food just because I was hungry; I think the last person to do so was my Mom, and since she was my friend too, even that hadn't counted.

I wondered if getting away from it all would someday turn me into a nice person, too, and I also wondered if it meant I would eventually stop wearing shirts and shoes for good. And that's what Chester claimed, that he'd been barefoot and shirtless for going on seven years running now, and that he had no intention of ever donning them again. I didn't see how it was possible in the modern age to go totally without either, let alone to stay warm enough, but I wasn't going to doubt a man who had just given me crispy, spicy, blackened grilled fish straight from the ocean.

It did turn out however that Chester had more than enough fish to be handing it out willy-nilly; an entire freezer full of it in fact. Not that it made him less of a decent guy to do so. But Crazy Chester was also *Captain* Chester, skipper of the charter fishing boat

S.S. Lazy Lizard, moored a short distance away in the harbor. The boat had come with the bar, which had been a pleasant surprise to Chester, who hadn't even known he owned it until the harbormaster came by and asked if he was going to move it during a hurricane warning in 2002. She was called the Albatross at the time, but Chester had a grudge against sea gulls of any kind and immediately renamed her and painted her green. Soon after he began taking charters out deep sea fishing, but not before ordering a Frozen Concoction Maker to put on board, because, he said, the fish don't always bite, and it was one sure way of sending people home happy.

Captain Chester had been scheduled to take a couple out that very morning, but they were running late. Actually, they were late for being late for being late by now, having called twice to say they'd be there in a few minutes and still having not arrived. It meant they were going to have a shorter trip out than usual, and for the regular rate; they weren't getting any deals, because although Chester didn't mind waiting so much, he did mind paying his backup bartender slash deck swabber and his first mate slash fish cleaner when he didn't have to, and the two of them had been there since ten o'clock keeping themselves busy doing nothing down on the Lizard. But when I mentioned I'd never been out deep sea fishing before, Chester told me he'd be glad to take me along for half price since I hadn't pissed him off yet today. That and he hated going out alone with couples; he said they always either got along too well or too badly, and he liked having someone else to talk to.

It was only another forty-five minutes after a third phone call that Bill and Teri finally arrived. They didn't say why they were so late, but I could guess. Probably for no reason whatsoever, other than some people just don't perceive time the way the rest of us do. They're late for school, late for work, and late for picking you up. They'll probably be late for their own funeral, too, since a lot of them are so laid back, which is why they're always late to begin with. It bugs the hell out of the rest of us clock watchers, but they're never gonna change.

At least Bill and Teri seemed like genuinely nice people, and I'd never have been on board Chester's fishing boat, as I was now, if they hadn't made it late for departure to begin with. As we steamed out of the harbor I sat back and took it all in, and was reminded of the scene in *The Perfect Storm* when George Clooney is describing what it's like to do just that. There was no lighthouse, or lighthouse keeper's kid to wave at. And the fog had already lifted, if it had ever been there to begin with. And I didn't know a black back or herring gull from a dump duck, and I'm not sure Chester cared either since he was finger shooting at all of them as they circled his boat. But between the birds, the sun, the sound of the motor, and the sight, smell and feel of the ocean, I could have been Captain Billy Tyne. I guess at the least I was George Clooney at last, improvising a part in my own movie.

Once we got far enough out to sea and into one of Captain Chester's favorite spots, he baited us up and we dipped our hooks in the water and the waiting began. I soon realized that ninety percent of fishing on the ocean is the exact same as fishing on a lake; talking and drinking. And the main difference in the other ten percent is that the boat, bait, pole, fight, and fish are all bigger.

What really sets the two apart though are their respective ambiances. There's a quiet, serene peace to fishing on a glassy lake that you've gotta love. But the ocean is different; the peace I felt now was more, well, exciting. Or maybe adventurous is a better word. It might have been because it was my first time way out on the open sea, or Crazy Chester's Chesteritas, but I felt very much alive.

I felt even more alive, and envious, when we hooked our first fish. It bit on Teri's line; it was easy to tell who's, given the high pitched shriek of delight that pierced the salty air. She fought with it for a while and

I realized there was one more difference between the lake and out here; this was a lot more work. But eventually it paid off and she pulled a nice grouper out of the water.

Soon Bill did the same, and then again, and then back to Teri once more. I was beginning to think something fishy was going on; this was just the sort of activity I tended to get the short stick of, and I wanted my share of the action. True, I was getting the whale's share of the drinks this way, but I didn't know of any famous Hemingway stories called *"The young man and the Chesterita"*, and I guessed I wasn't living a classic sea faring tale in the making.

But at last I got my wish when something pounced and started running off with my line. Even though I'd been sitting there watching Teri and Bill pull in fish my mind went totally blank, and I suddenly had no idea what to do, other than panic. Luckily Teri started coaching me; I don't know if Papa Joe would have approved, but I have no problem with equality for women, and I'm especially not picky when I'm in dire need of help. Thanks to her I soon had things reasonably under control, and had fallen into a steady pull, then lower the rod and quickly reel in some line and repeat motion. I was amazed at how much leverage it took to gain ground, my last epic fishing battle having been with a sunfish I'd defeated with relative ease. I could tell I was gonna be sore the next day if I caught many of these sea faring fish, despite all the vigorous training I'd done over the last couple of weeks lifting bottles and glasses.

It took a while, but in the end I got the fish up to the back of the boat. I knew by then it was a Mahi-Mahi, or dolphin-fish (which didn't tell me much, other than that I'd recently eaten part of one of his many siblings). Captain Chester had identified its species when it had leapt out of the water. Eventually we got it on board, but not before our good captain leaned too far off the stern with the gaffing hook and promptly fell in the ocean, uttering a parting, *"Dang it!"* as he went. Once we fished him back out he didn't seem to mind, though, and said it happened to him all the time.

He was quite a sight to behold, my new finned friend. I'd never seen a fish this large out of the water before; thirty-seven inches long, and weighing in at twenty-two pounds. And he was so colorful, almost like a bird, covered in brilliant shades of green and gold. He reminded me of a short, slimy, big headed, painted for game day Packers fan.

Captain Chester asked me if I wanted to keep or release him, a question that hadn't occurred to me. But since I didn't have any place for the meat and they rarely mount real fish anymore and simply paint a replica to match, I didn't see the point in killing him even if it was my place in the food chain. Besides, Chester told me a dolphin-fish's colors fade to a dull silver gray when it dies, and that seemed sad, unless it was going to be gray in my belly where it didn't matter. So instead we took some pictures, and set him free to go make more little big fishies.

The rest of the trip out on the sea didn't matter. We caught some more fish, drank some more Chesteritas, and had a great time. But my first big catch was like my first lover; I wasn't sure if I was doing anything right at the time but it was a helluva lot of fun, and none of the others would mean quite the same, even if I eventually improved on my technique.

We pulled back into the harbor just before the sun went down, then watched it set from the bar's balcony over another round of Landsharks and non-sanctioned sandwiches. Not a bad day for the price of one unauthorized right turn. Like Jimmy says, take another road.

Chapter 27:
"One peculiar harbor."

I crossed that bridge when I came to it, and passed into the mystical land known as Key West. It was the culmination of my journey, the place I'd been looking forward to the most, and the end of the road. All I could do from here was turn around like Forrest Gump, and run all the way back in the other direction.

I had a hotel reservation thanks to Crazy Chester; I wouldn't have had a clue where to stay, but he told me about a place he liked that was right in the heart of Duval Street, the Southern Cross. The fact that Chester made his way down to Key West from time to time made me suspicious again at first about his no shoes and shirt forever philosophy, but I did find a number of bars and restaurants where he'd be able to pull it off, so who knows.

Once I said goodbye to Highway A1A and hit the roads leading into the heart of Old Town, I knew immediately that my car was not only going to be mostly unnecessary, but a downright pain in the ass. The streets were narrow, like they had been in New Orleans, built also it seemed with horses and buggies in mind. That was a cool thought, but not so cool for driving purposes. There were bicycles and scooters popping out of everywhere, as well as crazy taxi drivers (are there any other kind?) expertly weaving through the obstacles like Adrian Peterson. If you live on the island you probably get used to it, but it was difficult as a first time visitor to gawk at the sights and avoid having a moped as a hood ornament, and I was relieved when I found the hotel and managed to snag a parking spot.

The Cross was everything Chester had said it would be; nice, simple, clean, and quiet. And when I walked out the white picket fence gate onto Duval Street, I knew from asking the front desk clerk that Jimmy's Margaritaville was only a little over a block to the right, and that Captain Tony's was just a little over a block to the left. Decisions, decisions.

As usual my stomach won out; Captain Tony's didn't serve food, and as anxious as I was to finish my two thousand mile trip to go down and get out of the heat, my body needed fuel first. So right turn it was, and moments later I walked into the Jimmy joint where they'd all began.

Every Margaritaville is different and cool in its own way. The one in New Orleans for example, is as brightly colored as a Mardi Gras float. And the one at Universal Studios Orlando is *really* big, like the theme parks, bordering on massive. But I instantly loved the Key West oldest sibling the best. It's just so...Key West. It has a comfortable lived in feeling, like a pair of flip-flops you've had so long there's an indent of your feet worn in the soles. Don't get me wrong, the place is still very nice, and festive. It's just a seasoned veteran, and the room resonates with the vibes of thousands of Parrot Heads who've stopped in over the years for a good time.

I had a Cheeseburger in Paradise and a margarita, a combo I'd been saving for this location. Call it a lack original thinking if you want; I call it being sentimental. And it was my trip, and I was going to do whatever the hell I wanted with it, and what I wanted to do next after my sensuous treat was to see Captain Tony's Saloon. I left Margaritaville and hurried down Duval, something I was going to have to work on not doing, and found the bar around the corner on Greene Street. I ducked inside, and took a moment to look around.

There's a line in a Jimmy Buffett song where he talks about not trying to describe the ocean if you haven't seen it, and for good reason. My mind had had all sorts of images of what Captain Tony's would be like, and not one of them had been even close to reality. For example, I underestimated the number of bras that would be hanging from the ceiling by, oh, about one hundred. The same with the gazillion or so business cards that covered the walls. And for some strange reason I never pictured a tree in the middle of the room growing up and out of the roof. I don't know what I was thinking; it should have all been obvious. Now that I was actually there I wondered how I ever could have imagined it any differently.

I went up to the bar and pulled up a stool. They all had names of famous people painted on them who I assumed had sat there at one time or another. I had my choice between Arlo Guthrie and Robert Deniro; Arlo's stool seemed like the safe choice, but I sat on Deniro's anyway. Thankfully, *"Are you sitting on me?!"* didn't resonate beneath my cheeks.

I ordered a simple beer and sat drinking it while trying to get my brain into total shut down mode. This was it. The end of the trip, or at least the end of my plans. When I set out on my trek I'd had certain big goals in my mind, places I wanted to see, things I definitely wanted to do. I was going to go to New Orleans and have gumbo. Then I'd fly to Mexico and Jamaica and drink tequila and rum on their respective beaches. I wanted to spend a night at Jimmy's hotel in Pensacola, and I was going to drive all the way down to Key West and visit Margaritaville and Captain Tony's. Done, done, done, done done, done and done.

It was time to come to grips with the fact that I no longer had a plan. In an odd sort of way, my real attempt at living my life like a Jimmy Buffett song began now; the rest of the trip had been like a rookie training camp, teaching my mind and body about other ways of life that didn't involve fluorescent lights, freezing winters, sitting in front of a TV, or trying a *new* Applebees or TGIF's. Now it was time to step up to the plate and show I belonged in the big leagues of laid-backism.

It's an odd feeling, one that I doubt most people ever have, to know that in that moment there was absolutely *nothing* I had to do. There was no job, no girlfriend, no house to take care of, no fish to feed, not even a fern to water. I could walk out the door and go in any direction and do anything I wanted, or I could just sit there on Bobby until they threw me out the door. This state of nothingness I was experiencing wouldn't last forever of course; I'd have to plug back into some sort of monetary input eventually, and maybe fairly soon. But knowing you'll have to go to work somewhere someday doesn't feel nearly as confining as knowing you have to be back in the office next Monday.

I finished my beer and walked back out onto Duval and looked around; I'd seen Captain Tony's and though I could have happily sat there all day, I felt I should explore. There were plenty of places to head towards, and I stood there, puzzling over which way to go first. The fact of the matter is I don't work well without a program. That's the stupid irony of it all, my trying to live a spontaneous, unpredictable lifestyle. I always needed a plan, even if it was planning a way not to have a plan. This time I decided to enforce my M&M regiment.

I have this thing for blue peanut M&Ms; I always try to eat them first, then sulk when I'm left with only the other colors. They just taste better, I tell you. So I force myself to quickly look and grab the first M&M I see, no matter what the color. It's a bit of a compromise, since my eye has a tendency to head straight to the blue ones anyway, but it cuts down a little on the blue genocide rate.

That was what I was going to do now in Key West; I'd simply keep my head down until I got outside of wherever I was, then look up and head into the very first place I saw that I hadn't been to yet. Silly, I know, but I wanted my first day in Key West to be as random as possible.

So for the next eight hours I was a tiny boat bobbing merrily along the rivers and tributaries that made up the mighty Old Town alcoholic waterway. The eddies and currents took me to established ports such as Sloppy Joe's and Hog's Breath, as well as tiny, peculiar little harbors like the Smallest Bar in Key West. Occasionally I got stuck in a whirlpool of fun that took some time to float back out of, like at Irish Kevin's; music, laughs, and beer can make for strong currents. But eventually I floated back out the door and into the main stream.

By the end of the night I was tacking fiercely to make any headway, and listing badly to my port side. I had taken on a fair amount of water, or at least some other sort of liquid with a slightly more complex molecular structure that seemed to affect my steering. I was beginning to get that sinking feeling and was worried that I might soon toss out my anchor if my voyage didn't end soon, when I spied the yellow neon of the Southern Cross Hotel sign on the horizon. I checked my phone; it was only eleven o'clock, but I was on Key West Duval Crawl time, and my tiny ship was already thoroughly tossed. It was time for this sailor to navigate safely back to his home port and bunk while he could still read the stars and walk at the same time.

I vowed that tomorrow I'd settle down and explore what the island had to offer besides way too many great bars for its own good, and take it easy until late afternoon or so. But a Bloody Mary to start the day wouldn't hurt. Or two. And maybe a cold beer with lunch. And a mango daiquiri during my travels might be nice.

I'd be good, though, I told myself. Just wait and see.

Yeah, right.

Chapter 28:
"Me went down and talked to I."

The Blue Heaven. The Green Parrot. The Schooner Wharf Bar. I could go on and on, and I did. It took me three days of good intentions to even start to begin to behave; but I swear it was the island's fault, not mine. I'd get up and wander around, pop into a store or two, maybe a small museum, walk along the waterfront. Then I'd get hungry and stop into some little open air place that had live music and have myself a conch sandwich, or some other such delicacy. And I'd have a strawberry margarita, or a mango daiquiri, or just about anything else you could shove into a blender and blend. The music would be playing, the ocean breeze would be breezing, I'd get knee deep in conversation with a local or tourist, and four hours and no good reason to move later, I'd finally go stumbling back out in search of a different place to be sedentary in. I was stuck in a vicious cycle of relaxation.

But on the fourth day I finally put my flip-flop down, and demanded I take a break and try and figure out what I was going to do with the rest of my time on Earth. And while part of me insisted that what we'd been up to lately seemed like a great way to spend eternity, I wasn't sure the song I'd been searching for was entitled *"My mojitothon"*, no matter how seductive and delicious the minty little fiends I was becoming addicted to were.

So against the heavy protests of the Party party, who had gained so much political clout in my body, I put that body in a taxi and drove it straight over to Smather's Beach, and parked it on a lounge chair facing the ocean to think.

I kicked back in the tropical sun, and tried to figure out what new tunes I might have learned over the last few weeks of travel. Firstly, I decided that having a good time was a good time, and that I had no intention of ever totally stopping again. I was also willing to bet that cutting loose kept you a lot younger than sitting at home vegetating in front of the TV, until you finally became one with your sofa. I didn't figure this was exactly an Earth shattering revelation, but it was more than I had known a little over a month ago. But now that *I* had the information, the question was, what to do with it.

I wasn't about to spend the rest of my life sitting in a bar drinking; they had names for people like that, and while being the wino that I'd know sounded cool in a song, I didn't think it would live up to the glamor in reality. But being someplace where going out on the town for the evening became something special was a must. Or maybe even more so, for the afternoon, since

I'd found that being a night owl in the sunshine was even better. I wanted ambiance so fine to go with my boat drinks, and a climate where the temperature outside wasn't sometimes colder than that of those same frozen concoctions.

My train of thought got derailed by something shiny, when two bikini clad lovelies showed up and began frolicking on the beach. Actually they weren't doing much frolicking, but they were definitely shiny, lying there glistening with coconut oil under Sol. When I paired the view with the soundtrack that was being provided by the breeze rustling through the palm trees above me, I felt like I was inside of yet another Corona commercial, except the prop boy hadn't handed me my ice cold bottle with lime yet. Mm, Corona...

The conductor gave the orchestra in my head a few terse taps on the podium to get its attention again, and I tried to remember what I'd just been thinking about. What it all boiled down to was, I didn't want it to end. Not so much all the festivities, but more so the way I felt. When I'd thought my life was about to be taken away by Old Man Winter, Peterbilt, and my own stupidity, it had seemed at the time like nothing more than the final annoyance. But it wouldn't have been the same, now; I liked living quite a bit again, thank you, and I didn't want to lose that.

It was probably a good sign, the fact that I wanted more of this life stuff. I was so buried up to my neck in self inflicted crap at the time of the accident that a few more inches up and over the top of my head didn't seem to matter that much. I'd hated my job at Image Makers, wasn't getting along with Brittany, and loathed and despised winter. When I quit all that and sold everything I owned and hit the road, I left behind my negative weight. Without it, my mood scale tipped towards the upbeat side at the slightest provocation. In other words, it was easy for me to be happy now because I didn't have any reason not to be.

And right now, it didn't hurt that I was in Key West, either. It had taken me all of about two hours to fall in love with the place, and it wasn't just because it had more great bars than any town should be allowed without coming with a warning sticker. Not that that wasn't a strong selling point, of course. It just wasn't the only thing that made me feel all warm and fizzy.

I loved that Key West was also an island. I'd already walked or biked from end to end and side to side a couple of times, and a finite habitat was very appealing. If I took off in any direction in Minneapolis, I would just find more of the same; more buildings, more roads, more ground. You could just keep going, which was great if you were Jack Kerouac. But this Jack Danielson guy, he was better off quickly running out of land to remind him there was no reason to go anywhere but where he was. And if you were going to be surrounded by something, what better something than a whole lot of Mother Ocean, who made the air taste sweeter and the view ever so more lovely? It beat the heck out of running into the Great Wall, that was for sure.

And then there were the people; a friendly bunch, these Conchs certainly were. A bit different, too, with philosophies that ranged from the norm to the crazy. I guess that's the same all over the world, just there seemed to be a higher percentage of Conch's who tended towards the crazy end, or at least most people's idea of crazy. And they didn't seem so hell bent on getting into each other's business as they do in more sane places, either, being more concerned with just livin' their own life. And that was a wonderful thing.

But the biggest reason I loved Key West was the one I couldn't put my finger on. It was that intangible feeling I got when I walked down the street, or sat on a bench and just observed. Jimmy talked about the songlines that he followed, and I think there must be thousands of them intersecting in Key West. The place really does sing to you, if you know enough to listen; it would be a perfect place to try and find one's own song, and maybe the right place for me to find mine.

So was that it? I loved where I was, so perhaps I should just try and put some roots down and see what happened? It seemed too simple. After the accident, I'd created this whole epic thing in my head, this grand treasure hunt for happiness. Yet as the days had gone by, the importance of all that had steadily melted away. It was hard to even recall now exactly why everything had seemed so complicated. Sitting here enjoying the sunshine was a more constructive way to spend my time than working out how to enjoy it, and napping in that same sun sounded even more constructive yet, since I could accomplish two things at once.

I let my mind wander off from the subject it was supposed to be focused on, like Spicoli on a hot California afternoon in Mister Hand's classroom, and felt my consciousness go in and out in the tropical heat. I was a little pooped from my festivities over the past few days, and I kept slipping into that weird little world where you aren't quite asleep and yet obviously not awake either, or you wouldn't be seeing rabbits or sea turtles out of the corner of your eye. Or, for that matter, George Clooney, coming towards you down the beach.

I'm not sure at what point I conched totally out, but I'm guessing it was somewhere between the dancing red iguanas and George. He walked up and pulled another lounger next to mine, but turned it the other way so he faced me, and sat down. His shirt, shorts, and flip-flops mirrored mine, so it was obvious he had good taste. Unfortunately it was also obvious he looked a lot better in them than I did, the bastard.

"Hey," said George.

"Hey," I said back.

"Nice day, isn't it?" said George.

"Yes, very nice," I said.

"Beats the hell out of standing in a snowdrift," he said, looking around him.

"How would you know?" I asked. "Get a lot of snow in Hollywood, do you?"

George shrugged. "Don't have a clue. Is there some reason you think I should?"

"Oh, I don't know...maybe because you're George Clooney?" I said.

"Sorry, but no I'm not," he said. "Him, I mean. Come on, you don't really think George Clooney would be caught dead in this ridiculous shirt, do you?"

"What's wrong with my shirt?" I said defensively, then shook my head. "Never mind. Look; if you're not George Clooney, then who the hell are you?"

"I'm you, dummy," he said.

"Me?" I said.

"Yes. Well, our projection of you anyway," me said. "We tend to exaggerate our looks, don't we?"

"Maybe a little," I said.

"More than a little," said me. "But now let's ask you a question; what the hell is our problem this time?"

"The same thing as always," I said. "My life, and what to do with it."

"Are we still going on about that? I would think it would be obvious by now," said me.

"Hey, if you know the answer, than tell me," I said. "I think it involves being right here, right where I am. But the rest..."

"There is no rest," said me. "That's it. Just get out there and live our life."

"I plan to, but *how*?" I said. "*How* do I do it and make sure I'm happy?"

Me sighed. "Sometimes I don't know why I waste my breathe on myself. Look; we keep acting like this is still our old life with the same old problems, but it's not. That life is dead and gone, and we get to start a brand new one. We've got a second chance, something most people never get. And we get to start out happy, without any baggage, like a new born baby. Just think of our accident as a rebirth," me said, standing up as if to leave.

"Wait, where are you going?" I said. "You can't leave already; we haven't figured anything out yet."

"I refuse to help us waste any more of our time when there's nothing wrong," me said. "We're already happy, Jack. Just don't rush us into anything now. Don't start us on some big new career just because we think we need one. And don't get us into some serious relationship with the first dame we meet."

"Dame?" I said. "You're Jack, remember, not George; Jack doesn't date dames."

"Sorry, got confused for a minute there. Although stepping up to a dame now and again might be kind of nice. Take care, Jack," me said, turning to leave.

"Hold it," I said. "Isn't there any way you could boil all this down to a simple philosophy? Something I can easily digest and use whenever I need to make a decision? You know, the sort of thing they might put on a motivational poster?"

Me looked irritated for a moment, then said, "Alright; just this one time, and then we're on our own." Me knelt down and whispered quietly in my ear, and when he was finished, I knew that he'd nailed it and that it was something I could use. It was simple, it was clean, and it was true. Well, most of it was clean, anyway.

"We're happy; life is a good thing. All we have to do now is not fuck it all up again."

And that was it at last. I knew what I had to do, or more importantly what I had to not do.

Thank you, mister other me.

Chapter 29:
"Gonna sing my own song."

I woke up in my little one room apartment above the Conch Shell Gift Shop on Duval Street in Key West, stretched, smiled, and got out of bed.

Even a little thing like that felt different now from how it had a few months ago. Then again, it *was* different.

The alarm wasn't going off, for one thing. In my old life, you weren't going to get me out of bed until the last damn second, when the electronic devil on my nightstand started screaming at me, and then usually nine minutes later. I just didn't see the point of being conscious for any longer in the AM than I had to, since all I had to look forward to was a crappy job, an often snowy world, and an annoying, not so nice, skinny blonde girlfriend. But that's changed now, and I can tell you without a doubt that not wanting to sleep away as much of the day as you can is the only way to fly. Although admittedly the occasional wake up in a hammock, sometime way past noon, does have its merits, too.

Of course, I still have to work like everyone else, so there are days I have to get up by a certain time. That can rarely be helped, but you can at least try to do something for boat drink funds that you enjoy more than running naked through a Mexican agave patch. For myself, I chose to get back to bar tending.

Yeah, it can almost be as prickly as a cactus sometimes when a New Yorker in a Hard Rock Cafe tee shirt keeps telling you again and again he wants a lime in his Cuba Libre. But it beats the hell out of sitting in a cubicle in an air conditioned office, pouring over bar graphs charting whether the blue flower or the red star in the corner of the ad made people more likely to buy your client's toothpaste. That kind of thing can drive you to drink, and I'd rather walk there, thank you.

But today I had the day off, so it was even better than the norm, which wasn't that bad to begin with. I got cleaned up, then went downstairs and strolled out onto Duval.

It made my heart sing a happy little tune whenever I opened that door at the bottom of the stairs and stepped onto the concrete sidewalk, knowing the delightful array of sights, sounds, smells, tastes, and sensations that were waiting for me in every direction. And all within a healthy walks distance.

Today I turned right, heading south. It was still morning, but the tourists were already in full force, probably disembarked from a cruise ship. They used to get on my few remaining nervous nerves even when I wasn't at work, but then one day I asked myself why I thought they shouldn't be here. I'd been a tourist once too, and not everyone can pick up and move to Key West; the island's not that big to begin with, so there's hardly space for the whole human race. But it's the kind of place that anybody with the proper mental longitude and moral latitude should have the right to see at least once in their lives, so visitors are all welcome as far as I'm concerned. And besides, three hundred and sixty-six or so bars would have a hard time surviving on the twenty-five thousand locals no matter how much they like to imbibe, and we wouldn't want to lose many of those, now would we?

My flip-flops guide me expertly on my way across the island; they're my GPS by now, and on some of my more free sailing nights are the only reason I find my way back home. They know these streets even better than I do, and always seem to take me to where I need to be, even if I didn't know I needed to be there.

This morning they took me to heaven; the Blue Heaven, that is. I needed sustenance to fuel my day, as well as a top-off on my soul. A short time later I was enjoying a glass of fresh squeezed with my rooster special, the chickens surrounding my table not seeming to mind that I was dining on their children. I didn't see any hummingbirds dancing in the trees today, but the cats snooping around, and the eclectic and beautiful backyard atmosphere, nicely made up for their absence.

Afterwards, I walked back to my apartment to get my old blue bike, and cycled over to Fort Zachary Beach. As usual I'd forgotten that the Heaven was on the way *to* the beach, so I had to backtrack to get my ride. But that was the way my mind worked, or didn't work, in Key West. It didn't seem overly concerned with remembering much of anything, and when it forgot, it didn't get all worked up about a few extra blocks of walking.

A couple of hours of lying in the sand on my Landshark beach towel by the ocean was more than enough to keep my skin aglow, and it allowed the salt air to start to stick to that skin. It also gave the sand a chance to migrate into several areas it didn't naturally belong, but being on the beach was a symbiotic relationship, and I'd grown to not mind. I'd come to think of each grain I carried away as a souvenir of time spent next to Mother Ocean, a tiny if sometimes chaffing keepsake of a magical place.

From there my bike and I just wandered for a while, down the narrow, flowered streets of Old Town. The tropical sun was really beginning to warm the day now, and I knew that despite the fact I was pedaling at a pace hardly faster than walking, I was going to work up a terrible thirst with all this near exercise. So before things got too out of control and I began to actually sweat, I made my way back to base camp and leaned my bike against the brick wall in the alley, and began the usual voyage north.

I stopped into the house that Buffett built, Margaritaville, and took a seat at the bar. I was in the mood for a mango daiquiri, and a little accompanying Jimmy sounds always made one go down even better. They were tricky, though, these frozen concoctions; if my taste buds had their way I'd down the thing in about a minute, and have nothing to show for it but an ice cream headache and an urge to order another. So I paced myself, interspersing sips with people watching, always a big league sport in Key West. But it was still over all too soon, like your first horizontal mambo.

My next port was supposed to be the Schooner Wharf Bar, but my flip-flops and I couldn't be bothered to walk the entire way in one whole six block trek, a distance that should never be attempted if there are friendly ports along the way. Ducking into Captain Tony's to get out of the heat, into Finnegan's Wake for a pint of stout and a discussion on the merits of football vs football, and finally Kermit's Key Lime Shoppe for a slice of pie never hurt anyone, including me. That was perhaps the greatest thing about Key West; no matter where you were going or how close your destination was, there were always things to distract you in between as you made your way there, and the journey often became the thing.

When I did finally arrive at the Schooner, Michael McCloud was in his usual spot up on the stage, singing his tunes and good-naturedly grumbling at the crowd. The Schooner Wharf Bar is, as one writer put it, the center of the universe. It's definitely mine, and for all the same reasons Key West is that I can't properly put into words. It's a feeling more than anything, and when I'm there, I'm like an octagon peg in an octagon hole, my many sides all fitting at last.

I sat down at my usual table in the shade, kicked off my flip-flops, and ordered a Kalik. And three hours later I was still there, although the Kalik was long gone, as well as several of his relatives. And I would have stayed even longer and into the night, but more music was calling across the island.

I'd dawdled for too long, as if that were possible, and had a quick eight block walk ahead of me to my destination. I tried to do it in one long march; I really did. But the Mojitos calling from the open doorway of the Lazy Gekko as I walked past nixed that plan, so by the time I reached the Green Parrot Bar, the band had already started its afternoon sound check show. They were a Cajun group down from the New Orleans area, and I hadn't wanted to miss them, so I was as mildly irritated as I get these days with my tardiness. I've been meaning to look into cloning so I can be in a bunch of different locations at once on the island, and do away with all this tedious walking from place to place, but haven't gotten around to it yet. Maybe tomorrow, if I find a spare moment in my busy schedule.

By the time the band finished under Smirk's watchful gaze, I'd worked up a sudden urge to see the sun set. That meant a trip back to the other part of the island again, but I didn't want to risk my flops becoming overheated and blowing out, so I treated myself to a taxi. I got to Mallory Dock with minutes to spare, grabbed some conch fritters from Mike's stand on the dock, and wandered through the crowd.

I stopped to watch three young guys defying gravity and the grim reaper on pogo sticks, then realized the day was getting close to last call. I dropped a buck in the trio's hat, the least I could do for risking life and limb to entertain me, then pushed my way expertly through the gawkers to a decent vantage point to watch for the green flash. I didn't see one, but I was treated to the sight of Sol sinking into Mother Ocean, sending a sparkling array of light across her waves, while a rainbow of colors painted the clouds above her. Not a bad way to spend a few moments of my existence.

The rest of my evening was the usual gumbo of adult fun. A glass of fine rum at the Rum Barrel, a fish sandwich in the castaway atmosphere at BO's Fish Wagon, more great music from Jimmie Parrish and the Ocean Waves Band amongst the dollar bills at Willie T's, and some bawdy laughs at Irish Kevin's. And Jimmy (and Jack), there was still so much I could have done.

By the time my head hit my pillow, my happy tank was overflowing and dribbling all over my sheets. But I didn't care; though it would have been nice to be able to scoop it up and save the excess for a rainy day, I didn't see many of those on my horizon. Not just because I was in Key West, although that certainly didn't hurt, but because I refused to participate in anything that made me unhappy. That may sound difficult, but a lot of what tends to make us miserable is self inflicted, whether we want to admit it or not, and we're the only ones with the power to change it.

I do have a letter sitting on my dresser that I'm debating whether I should open or not. It's from a lawyer, *rarely* a good thing, but it's also from di island, and that's *usually* a good thing. Maybe tomorrow I'll take it to the Schooner and open it in the presence of a Mojito; I don't think anything bad could come of it there with all the good juju my home within a home gives me. And if it is something bad, I can always chuck it in the ocean.

Today was just another in a series of first days of the rest of my life. So other than many more days of kickin' back in paradise, what lies in my future? I don't know. Don't really care anymore, either. I am where I am and that's all that I am. Right now is all that matters, and my continuing to be aware that I am alive in only a single moment caught between the ones behind and in front of me.

I still don't really know exactly what my song is though, and maybe I never will. I do know that the search is the important thing, to not waste your life living a tune that isn't your own. I've learned the melody of mine and can hum the refrain, but there's still a lot to be written. Until then, I"m gonna just keep on jammin'.

May you one day find your own song, and live it always.

The End

If you enjoyed this story and would like to follow
Jack's further adventures, please check out
"Jack And Di Rum Song"
&
"Let Di Song Of Change Blow Over My Head"
the 2nd and 3rd books in the Island Series,
available on Amazon in paperback and Kindle,
and Barnes and Nobles for the Nook.

The author's short and very unofficial guide to Key West.

Forward

Key West is a very special place for me. I've tried to come up with a way to describe the feeling I get when I'm there, and have failed miserably. Being on the island does something to my brain, exciting and calming me at the same time. It delights all five of my senses, and several that I didn't even know I had. There's just something about this touristy, bustling, eclectic little island town that always feels like home.

There are a lot of things to like about Key West. The ocean breeze, sandy beaches, palm trees; and the weather, of course. The average annual temp is 77.8 degrees, making it the warmest city in America. Yet the hottest day on record is only 100 degrees. And the coldest day? 41 degrees. So if you're keeping score and are in the market for a moderate climate, the biggest temperature swing you're likely to get in Key West is 59 degrees. Back in Minneapolis, near to where this author hails from, it's 149 degrees, second only to Mercury in our solar system for extremes.

Key West is older than you may think; so much so in fact that they actually designate the historic western half of the island Old Town. Of course the city has its McDonald's and Super Americas. And they have a Kmart, although Walmart has yet to gain a foothold on the island. But many of the narrow streets are lined with buildings that have been there for a hundred years or more, and a simple walk can become a little journey into pleasing architectural aesthetics.

Another joy I've found in Key West is the people, a wonderful collection of eccentrics from all over the country and the world. Maybe it's because of the weather, but they're some of the friendliest folks I've ever run into. Perhaps the simplicity of life on the island also helps keeps everyone in a good mood, along with the feeling you are cut off from all the bull shit happening up in the continental United States. And why not? After all, why should the Conch Republic care what goes on in some foreign country?

And speaking of bars, or at least reasons why everyone is so happy in Key West, there are more than a few of them to be found on the island. How many you ask? Well, a taxi driver once told me there were three hundred and sixty-six; one for each day, including leap year. I don't know if that's true or not, but if anyone wants to give me a grant I'd be more than happy to do a study and get back to you. I can tell you for sure there are a helluva lot of them, and most are different and unique in some way.

So since this book is somewhat of a tribute to Jimmy Buffett and the Parrot Head lifestyle, it seems like the bar and restaurant scene would be a good place to start and focus almost entirely on in my little guide, which I'm writing as a nod and thank you to the places I've personally enjoyed in Key West. Keep in mind, this is all stuff *I* like, and that my list is by no means meant to be comprehensive. There are so many hidden gems to be found throughout the island, and the upper keys as well. I'm still discovering them myself, which is just another treat to the area.

Here then, starting with the bars, is my tiny little guide to Key West. I don't think it'll have *Fodor's* shaking in their boots, but I hope repeat visitors find a new place to check out, and that it gives first time visitors a few ideas on where to begin. And better still, I hope it makes a few people who have never been to Key West get off their lazy arses and get on a plane, because you people don't know what you're missing.

Sloppy Joe's

Located on Duval right in the heart of the action, Sloppy Joe's is probably the most famous bar in Key West, and the one tourists flock to first; but don't hold that against it. It's actually a great bar, big, wide open, and woody, decorated with pictures of Hemingway, fish, and Air Force memorabilia. Their signature drink is the Sloppy Rita, a top shelf marg with a couple of twists. The staff has always been good when I've been there, and they have a wide variety of live entertainment.

The bar's biggest claim to fame is that it's the watering hole Ernest Hemingway used to frequent and write in, but there's some debate on the matter. The story I've heard is that the original Sloppy Joe's was actually at the location where Captain Tony's is now, and due to a rent increase the bar staff and patrons simply picked up the furniture and their drinks one night, and moved the bar down the street to its present home. By the way, carrying your drinks from place to place is still allowed in Key West, so if you want to do a reenactment of the famous bar move from Tony's to Sloppy's be my guest; just don't try and take the furniture with you.

Captain Tony's

As I said before, this is probably the original Sloppy Joe's, but honestly, it doesn't matter one way or the other. Captain Tony's has its own claim to fame anyway, the late Tony Tarracino, the former owner who passed away in 2008. Captain Tony was the quintessential Key Wester, a man who lived one of those lives that are almost too unbelievable for the movies. He spent time as a saloon keeper, shrimper, gun runner, gambler, and eventually even Mayor of Key West, and of course, was a good friend of Jimmy Buffett. I, like so many others, met Captain Tony on a couple of occasions at the bar. He was often there signing t-shirts and chatting with customers, always wearing a warm smile. His mayoral slogan sums up his life best, I suppose; *"All you need in this life is a tremendous sex drive and a great ego; brains don't mean shit."*

As for the bar itself, that is precisely what it is; a bar. I would almost call it a dive bar, but some people might take that as an insult when it's not meant to be. They don't serve food, and I'm not sure they bother with TVs for sports. If they do, they're hiding somewhere. But those are all good things. There aren't enough bar bars left in the world, let alone unique ones. And Captain Tony's is unique. Painted pitch black, the walls and support beams are covered with thousands of business cards and IDs, so bring something to leave behind; I have at least two there that I can still find. The ceiling around the bar has hundreds of bras hanging from it too, so if you want to leave anything else behind...

The bar stools all have names painted on them of famous people who's cheeks have graced them; I always try to sit on John Candy. You can get your drink in a sturdy, refillable, souvenir plastic cup, with a picture of Captain Tony on it that actually looks just like my father. I have about forty of these by now, and they're the perfect glass for libations on a boat or pontoon since they're cool, hold a lot, won't break, and are wide bottomed and therefore harder to spill (but never impossible). Tucked away just off Duval down Greene Street, look for Captain Tony's big yellow sign with the giant fish.

The Green Parrot

Music; that's what the Green Parrot is all about. This excellent bar gets great bands from all over the south, playing original bluegrass, rock, Cajun, and everything else in and not between. There's a scattering of performances throughout the week, with music pretty much every Friday, Saturday and Sunday, the biggest treats being the 5:30 soundcheck shows; there's nothing better than a live band and cold beer while the sun is still shining.

The bar is famous for its jukebox, reputed to be one of the very best in America. I haven't had time to compare them all yet, which is the only reason I use the word *reputed*. It's damned fine, I know that much. Jammed with one hundred great rock and blues CDs, some fairly obscure, the jukebox even has its own page on the Parrot website so you can go in and check out what's playing, as if it were its own stage. And man, that would be quite the stage.

Decorated in a great all over the place style with local artwork and signs, the room's look is dominated by two things; one, a giant, silk parachute that hangs from the ceiling above the main bar. And two, the large, infamous painting of Smirk that watches over the patrons, making sure none of them are snivelling (and at the Parrot it *is* snivelling that's not allowed, not sniveling).

The Green Parrot is a place that no one, especially any self respecting music lover, should miss. But many people do, which I'm sure suits its local patrons just fine. Located barely out of the tourist zone, many Duval crawl folks never come across it. But it's only a short hop away from Jimmy's Margaritaville, one block south, then one block west on Southard. Take the extra steps and give your ears a treat; but don't snivell, or you'll have to answer to Smirk.

Finnegan's Wake

I've been to a number of Irish pubs throughout the years and I have to say Finnegan's is my favorite. It's one of those places you don't expect to find in Key West; at least I didn't, and whenever I walk through the frosted doors on the corner of James and Grinell Streets I feel like I've been suddenly transported off the island. Normally that would be a bad thing, but in Finnegan's case it's worth the trip.

If you're a diehard sit outside type of vacationer, Finnegan's has a very nice backyard patio bar. But I head for the pub inside, which is so traditionally Irish I'm surprised there aren't leprechauns in flip-flops sitting on booster seats drinking pints at the bar. It's a beautiful place, and a welcome sanctuary from the heat on a hot day.

For lovers of great beer I'm not sure there's a better place in Key West than Finnegan's; they have a fantastic and constantly evolving selection of bottles and barrels from around the world. And happy hour is something you don't want to miss; it's so nice to find a place that doesn't penalize you for drinking real beer. The last time I visited I had a pint of delicious porter for a couple of pounds, er dollars.

Finnegan's does have live music, too, and excellent traditional Irish cuisine. But you'll need to change your routine if you're strictly a Duval crawler and want to visit; it's nestled in a quiet neighborhood about five blocks to the east. Just look for the nice white building on the corner with the Irish flags.

The Smallest Bar in Key West

This is one of those places you find all over Key West, somewhere just a little bit different from the norm. I'm not sure how many times I walked past before I noticed it, squeezed in between two buildings on the north end of Duval. Technically it's part of the Old Customs House Inn to which it's adjacent, though it looks more like someone just set up a bar at the end of a narrow alley. And if it is an alley it's one of the more colorfully decorated ones I've ever hung out in.

The Smallest Bar in Key West is just that; the name is no exaggeration. I've worked behind bars that are bigger than the whole place. The room, alley, or whatever you'd like to call it is about six feet wide by maybe eight feet long, and there are four bar stools, I think. It's a favorite photo opportunity, and if you look on the internet you'll find plenty of pictures of happy, drunken partiers squeezed into its confines. And why not; it's the smallest bar in Key West!

The staff, if one bartender constitutes a staff, is friendly, and they have a full service bar and a decent enough selection of reasonably priced beers. Be sure to stop in for a beverage and a photo as you make your way down Duval, but if you're in a group of ten or more be prepared to either take turns, or get to know each other very well.

Hog's Breath Saloon

Hog's Breath is another of the bars clustered right in the heart of Old Town. Though not technically on Duval, you can spot it through a parking lot next to Ripley's Museum and crawl right on over. Otherwise you can find it at its official 400 Front Street entrance.

Every bar in Key West seems to have one thing it's famous for; at the Hog's Breath Saloon it's their motto. Available on a wider selection of t-shirts than at any other place in town, it's funny because it's true; *"Hog's breath is better than no breath at all."*

But the Hog is more than just a saying. Most of the seating is outdoors, though they do have an indoor section as well. The outdoor area has three great features. One, good live music; there's someone playing pretty much all day from 1pm until close. Two, the raw bar; I personally haven't acquired a taste for the clammy little buggers, but it's there for those who have. And three, well, it's outdoors, as I said, and in Key West that's always a plus.

You can end up walking for miles in Key West if you're not careful, so it's best to do it in small increments and from bar to bar; Hog's Breath is another pleasant place to take a load off your flip-flops. And if you're hungry on your journey they serve a full menu, with everything from chilli to full dinners.

Irish Kevin's

Irish Kevin's is as often as not my last stop on a day of revelry in Key West. I didn't plan it that way at first, it just kept happening. I'd go in early in the evening and come out hours later when I was good and ready to collapse in my bed. Now I've more or less stopped fighting it, and head over when I'm sure I'm done with everywhere else.

The reason I keep ending up barnacled to my bar stool is pure and simple; good, rowdy fun. Kevin's always has entertainment, and most of the performers are good musicians and funny comedians. Many take great joy in giving audience members a hard time, and who doesn't love watching someone else get made fun of? One of the masters who's been at Kevin's for years now is Jared Michael Hobgood; be sure to check the schedule to see when he's playing, but don't shy away from the other acts either. Most are very entertaining.

There's usually some dancing going on, and the crowds can get pretty large. Irish Kevin's is a big place right on Duval Street near Sloppy Joe's, that's decorated just as its name implies. If you can't find it just close your eyes and listen for the sound of music, shouting and laughter; follow it, and most likely it will lead you straight to Kevin's.

Bo's Fish Wagon

Bo knows...something; I just have a hard time putting my finger on what it is. The owner's name is Buddy Owens, which is where the Bo part comes from, and it's another of those places that are so hard to describe and do justice to that I love so much.

Bo knows fish, I know that much. The wagon serves delicious fresh fish sandwiches on Cuban bread, as well as a smattering of other appetizers, sandwiches, and platters. But though the food is good it's the atmosphere that is unforgettable. Part Robinson Crusoe and part Gilligan's Island, the place looks like it was built entirely from whatever washed up on shore. That is, as long as a rusty pickup with a giant fish in the back could wash up on shore. Nets, nautical paraphernalia, quirky signs, bicycles; Bo's has that wonderfully thrown together shipwreck look that peppers Key West.

Bo's has live entertainment from time to time, including their Friday night jam session. The place can really get rocking and jammed with people, and is a local crowd favorite. You can find it in the corner of the parking lot at Caroline and William Streets, about three blocks east of Duval.

The Rum Barrel

As any self respecting pirate will tell you, rum is good. But in most of the bars in the U.S., you're likely to find only Captain Morgan, Malibu, and Bacardi, and perhaps Myer's or Appleton's as *special* rums, while thirty seven different types of vodka take up space on the shelf. Not so at the Rum Barrel, where rum is king. They offer one hundred different varieties, and you can even do a four rum sampler. Just paging through the *Rum Bible* is a treat, and can be a great learning tool to any budding buccaneers in need of initiation into the spicy, sugary, sometimes dark world of rum.

The Rum Barrel is a great place to watch sports, too. I've been there for football games, and each of the high-def TVs strategically placed around the bar has a sign with the time and game it will be showing. But Cowboys, Redskins, and Giants fans be warned; this is definitely an Eagles port. The owner hails from Philadelphia, and there's usually a rather boisterous pack of Eagle's fans during their games (and Phillies fans during baseball season). So be prepared for some good natured ribbing if you choose to fly a rival fleet's colors.

Serving an extensive menu ranging from tasty buffalo wings to lobster pot pie, the Barrel has both bar and restaurant seating, as well as live entertainment Tuesday through Saturday nights on the Quarterdeck, a very nice rooftop bar overlooking Old Town. All this plus good beer on tap, many special events, and of all things in a rum bar, a pirate motif. How can ye go wrong, mateys? Located one block east of Duval on Front Street.

.

Lazy Gecko

The Lazy Gecko is just a small, simple bar on Duval Street, down the road a few steps from Sloppy Joe's. But what sets it apart from many other similar type places is that everything they do, they choose to do right. The Gecko's specialty food wise, and one of the main reasons I keep popping back in the door, is their big, delicious, cold sandwiches. My personal favorite is the Gunny; smoked turkey breast, Gouda cheese, and spicy mangrove mustard on a tasty roll, served with chips and a huge dill pickle. Great eats and great ballast on a warm afternoon.

Decorated in a woody, colorful, tropical style, the Gecko has fourteen high-def TVs for the game, and they often squeeze a good small or one man band into the room for music in the afternoon. They do a nice happy hour every day from 5-8, extended on Sundays and Mondays, with great wing specials and 2 for 1 drinks. And if you like Mojitos, they have an extensive menu with a lot of choices to become addicted to.

Grab a table up by the entrance and you'll be only a step away from the sidewalk; it's a great place to just kick back and watch the Duval carnival go by.

Jack Flats

Jack Flats is a bar restaurant set more or less right across the street from Margaritaville, towards the quieter southern end of Duval. It's a very nice place, done in dark woods with a huge bar running along one wall. And it's air conditioned, making it a welcome hideout *if* you should ever get tired of the tropical heat.

I've had nothing but good, friendly service at Jack's, but then again that seems to be the norm in Key West, especially the friendly part. The place is filled with big screen TVs, especially towards the back where it opens into a larger room still, making it one of the best spots on the island to watch sports.

What sets Jack's apart for me is the food. Not that I've tried everything on their menu, mind you, 'cuz I can't seem to get past the few items I'm hooked on. They have the typical island offerings; good burgers, fish sandwiches, salads and appetizers. But they also offer what used to be called blue plate specials; my favorite is the pot roast, steaming piles of delicious shredded beef served with a mountain of mashed potatoes and gravy, and a side of veggies. After clearing a plate of that or the meatloaf, my ballast tank is nicely filled for the long haul. I also love their Philly sandwich, which may be the best I've ever had. Jack's is just a good place to get some tasty, hearty food.

Caroline's

Caroline's is an outdoor cafe on Duval near Caroline Street, and no, I haven't seen a woman going crazy around there...yet. It's another of my favorite places to eat, a perfect combination of tasty food and great atmosphere. And it's located right in the heart of my stomping/stumbling grounds, making it an easy place to stop into when my stomach starts petitioning for food.

They have a very extensive menu, serving up such items as their famous fish sandwich, spicy Cajun jambalaya, and Kingston jerk chicken served with black beans and fried plantains. And if you're in the mood for something simple, you can't go wrong with the huge Reverend Joe burger, or one of the items like Tex-Mex rolls or Dolphin fingers from their large selection of appetizers.

Caroline's is a great place to people watch if you can get a table by the street, which isn't always easy due to the brisk business they do. But if you can't, don't fret it, and just kick back and enjoy the garden atmosphere. You're in Key West, and you're outdoors; every little thing is gonna be alright.

Jimmy Buffett's Margaritaville

This is where they all began, the oldest sibling of the Margaritaville restaurant family. Like all Margaritavillle's it has the same three features; festive Jimmy Buffett atmosphere, good eats and drinks, and a store to buy Parrot Head goodies.

The Key West location fits the island perfectly, woody and worn after 25 years of operation. Located a few blocks south of the gaggle of bars in the heart of Old Town, it's the perfect place to take a load off on the way to or back from the Green Parrot or Blue Heaven.

The menu is quite large, offering for example Jamaica Mistaica wings, Andouille sausage with red beans and rice, Calypso mahi-mahi, BBQ ribs, and a Cuban sandwich. And then of course there's always the Cheeseburger in Paradise, done just like the song.

The bar has a nice selection, and the blenders are always working overtime (I sometimes wonder just how many gallons of margaritas they serve a year). There's good live entertainment every evening except Mondays, and you never know; there's always that tiny little chance Jimmy will stop by for an impromptu show.

Schooner Wharf Bar

Ah, the Schooner. There are a few places my body has inhabited that I absolutely love, where I always wish the day would never come to an end. The sand bar on Gull Lake in northern Minnesota, where everyone pulls up their boats and socializes, is one; the Schooner Wharf Bar in Key West is another.

Voted best locals bar six years running, the Schooner is a large, nautical themed outdoor bar partially covered by a roof. It's located next to the historic Key West Seaport, and offers a nice view of the yachts and tall ships moored there. My spot is the first picnic table under the roof, facing the stage, back bench, outside seat, flip-flops kicked off, with a bucket of Kalik beers in front of me. If it turns out we get to pick our own personal heaven, that's where you'll be able to find me.

The Schooner has great food, with one of the larger menus I've found in Key West. Tuna nachos, fish tacos, red snapper Reubens, Cuban mojo marinated mahi-mahi; the specialty here is seafood. But the burgers and jerk chicken are no slouches either, and I counted seventeen different appetizers the last time I checked, enough to keep you nibbling for hours. And if you're up early in the morning, the Schooner does a great breakfast, too.

As for entertainment, there's almost always something happening on the Schooner's stage. The main event though is Michael McCloud, a singer, songwriter, story teller who plays from noon until 5 PM every day but Monday. His music is great, but it's just as much fun listening to him tell his stories, or grouse at the crowd; paying attention to the entertainer seems to be a dying art, but Michael refuses to go down without a fight, and isn't exactly shy in his opinions. There are also good bands every night as well a talented and funny magician, Frank Everhart, who sets up in a corner of the bar virtually every evening.

The staff is excellent, and a few of the servers I've had have been among the best I've encountered anywhere; I'm a sucker for a waitress who pulls a fresh beer from my bucket and zips it into my bottle koozie for me without my asking. And for that small world feeling I even ran into a gal working there from my northern Minnesota lakes area stomping grounds.

The Schooner's slogan is *"Hang with the big dogs"* because the bar is canine friendly, so feel free to bring Fido; there'll usually be a few new tails for him to sniff.

The Schooner is a Key West original and the one place you don't want to miss during a visit; trust me.

Blue Heaven

The Blue Heaven is indeed a little plot of heaven. Set off the beaten Duval track, you actually have to make an effort to find it, thereby earning it. But a walk in Key West isn't such a bad thing, and getting to Heaven is worth it.

Most of the restaurant is set in a large, green courtyard filled with colorfully painted tables and chairs. Cats roam the area, as well as the famous roosters and chickens that mingle under the tables. Eclectic is definitely the key word here, and it's one of those places you simply have to see to fully appreciate.

I love having my breakfast at the Blue Heaven; the combination of food and atmosphere is just the perfect way to start the day. Banana pancakes with real slices of banana, or pineapple or pecan, freshly squeezed OJ, and the Rooster Special. Walk in dragging from the night before, and you'll walk back out ready to do it to yourself all over again.

Lunch and dinner are equally delicious; try the 12 herb spiced Jamaican jerk chicken sandwich for lunch, and the Caribbean BBQ shrimp, deglazed with Red Stripe Beer and served with brown rice and black beans for dinner. But leave a little room because the Blue Heaven has just about the best Key Lime pie on the island, if not the world.

Willie T's

For some reason it took me a while to discover Willie T's. But it also took only one visit for it to become one of my favorites. So I've only been to Willie's a couple of times, but I've already heard a ton of good music there. And the atmosphere? It's worth about a million bucks. Okay, maybe not that much, but it's well into the thousands. Like the business cards that cover Captain Tony's interior, Willie T's is *covered* in dollar bills; even the trees are coated with them. Besides all the dineros to look at it's also an open air establishment, so again, it's hard to go wrong.

They have two seating areas, one with clothed tables, and the other, well, typical Key West, comfortable as an old flip-flop, casual. Willie's has a big menu, full of good eats like thin crust pizza, pasta, jerk chicken, 2/3 pound burgers, and paninis.

Located just south of Margaritaville on the same block, you can find Willie T's and all that cash at 525 Duval.

Sunset celebration at Mallory Square

There's probably no one thing in Key West that says more about the island than the sunset celebration held every afternoon to evening down at Mallory Square. For one thing, how many places are there on Earth where you'd even bother to schedule an outdoor party every day, optimistic that it wouldn't get rained out? And how many cities have enough people who wouldn't get sick to death of doing the whole thing day after day for it to keep on truckin' year after year? Not many.

The celebration, which consists of arts and crafts stands, street performers, and food and drink, has been a happening thing in one form or another since way back in the sixties. It started as a meeting place for some of the hippies on the island who would gather and watch for Atlantis to arise out of the clouds, with a little chemical help, of course. And I think there may be a hippie or two who's still down on the dock, patiently waiting.

Many of the performers are quite good, while some are just getting their act together, so to speak. I've seen jugglers, comedians, trained cats, magicians, human statues, and uni-cycling dogs, amongst other acts. It's a great place to just wander around and see what you happen to see.

And then of course there's the sunset, which seems to go off like clockwork every day. And there's something magical about watching the sun set over the ocean, an ocean filled with clipper ships, yet. And there's always the hope that today will be the day you'll finally get to see that green flash.

One last note; for my money the best conch fritters in Key West are to be found at Mallory Square during the celebration. I don't know how Mike, the owner, beats all the island kitchens cooking out of his little stand, but he does. Mike's fritters are crunchy, fluffy,and delicious. And be sure to have a glass of his tasty key lime ice tea to wash them down.

Jolly II Rover

The Jolly II Rover is one of those tall ships you see sailing around near Mallory Dock. They do a two hour sunset cruise that I think is one of the better bargains in Key West, and you can bring your own food and beverages on board.

If you've been to Key West before you've probably taken pictures of the ships; the Jolly Rover is the pretty green and white schooner with the red sails. It's the only ship I've been out on so far, so it's the only one I can recommend. I'm not saying the other sunset ships don't do a great job, only that the Rover does.

You can help out the crew during the voyage if you like, or you can just sit back and relax. The captains I've had have been very knowledgeable about the area they sail through, and they and the crew have always been very friendly. And what's even more important to a prate like me, I *think* the Rover is the only sunset boat with working cannons...

Reservations can be made by phone, online, or by stopping at the booth they have in the Historic Key West Seaport. Take a two hour timeout for a sail, and you'll be rewarded with an experience you won't soon forget.

And one last thing...

My Key West Vacation Song
Written by Anthony Bjorklund (and just waiting to be recorded.)

Mahi-mahi and Caribbean rum,
A bottle of Kalik in the setting sun.
I love Key West, it's my home away from home.
Some day I'm gonna move down, and never ever roam.

The Green Parrot Bar, with its jukebox so fine,
Schooner Wharf Bar, where the dogs never whine.
Captain Tony's, and Sloppy Joe's,
Which one was first, god I really don't know.

Mahi-mahi and coconut rum,
A couple of Kaliks in the midday sun.
Would somebody thank Jimmy Buffett for me,
For singing songs that brought me to my island in the sea.

A Blue Heaven breakfast will make you feel good,
Even if you drank a little more than you should,
At Irish Kevin's and the Hog's Breath Saloon,
Doin' the Duval Crawl, under a Key West moon.

Mahi-mahi and Jamaican rum,
A bucket of Kaliks in the noonday sun.

The Conch Republic is the country for me,
I'd gladly pledge allegiance to old Captain Tony.

Michael McCloud sings me that Key West song,
I get my fritters on the dock and I can't go wrong.
I stumble 'round Old Town drinkin' beer after beer,
Then it's off to the Southern Cross before I fall on my
rear.

Mahi-mahi and any old rum,
Too many Kaliks and just way too much fun.
It's the Conchs down in Key West that'll make you feel
right,
I felt right at home on my very first night.

One week a year, man, it just ain't enough,
And Minnesota winters can get pretty rough.
Someday I'll go down til the end of me,
And live the easy life on this westernmost key.

I'll get my mahi-mahi and Jamaican rum,
A couple of Kaliks in the noonday sun.
Look out old Key West, I'll be coming your way,
And you'll have to put up with me every single day.

Made in the USA
Lexington, KY
11 June 2014